"Somebod
mis

Mikky raised her eye
hear it's bad luck to

"Guess this means I have to kiss you."

"Guess so," she whispered as Tony lowered his
lips.

Feeling dazed, Mikky drew her mouth slowly
away from his. For a man who was trying to keep
his emotional distance, he'd certainly leapt over
the chasm when he kissed her.

Mikky took a deep breath. "I don't know about
you, but that's one tradition I think the world
should really keep."

"Michelle…"

"Shh." She placed her fingertips to his lips to still
them. "I'm not asking you for anything, just to
enjoy the moment."

"You really are something else, aren't you?"

Mikky looked at him significantly. "Not better, not
worse, just something else." It was up to Tony to
realize just what that actually meant to him.

Dear Reader,

The end of the century is near, and we're all eagerly anticipating the wonders to come. But no matter what happens, I believe that everyone will continue to need and to seek the unquenchable spirit of love…of *romance*. And here at Silhouette Romance, we're delighted to present another month's worth of terrific, emotional stories.

This month, RITA Award-winning author Marie Ferrarella offers a tender BUNDLES OF JOY tale, in which *The Baby Beneath the Mistletoe* brings together a man who's lost his faith and a woman who challenges him to take a chance at love…and family. In Charlotte Maclay's charming new novel, a millionaire playboy isn't sure what he was *Expecting at Christmas*, but what he gets is a *very* pregnant butler! Elizabeth Harbison launches her wonderful new theme-based miniseries, CINDERELLA BRIDES, with the fairy-tale romance—complete with mistaken identity!—between *Emma and the Earl*.

In *A Diamond for Kate* by Moyra Tarling, discover whether a doctor makes his devoted nurse his devoted wife *after* learning about her past.… Patricia Thayer's cross-line miniseries WITH THESE RINGS returns to Romance and poses the question: Can *The Man, the Ring, the Wedding* end a fifty-year-old curse? You'll have to read this dramatic story to find out! And though *The Millionaire's Proposition* involves making a baby in Natalie Patrick's upbeat Romance, can a down-on-her-luck waitress also convince him to make beautiful memories…as man and wife?

Enjoy this month's offerings, and look forward to a new century of timeless, traditional tales guaranteed to touch your heart!

Mary-Theresa Hussey

Mary-Theresa Hussey
Senior Editor, Silhouette Romance

Please address questions and book requests to:
Silhouette Reader Service
U.S.: 3010 Walden Ave., P.O. Box 1325, Buffalo, NY 14269
Canadian: P.O. Box 609, Fort Erie, Ont. L2A 5X3

THE BABY BENEATH THE MISTLETOE

Marie Ferrarella

Silhouette

R O M A N C E™

Published by Silhouette Books

America's Publisher of Contemporary Romance

To
Mary-Theresa Hussey,
for reuniting me with
the Marino-McClellan Clan.
Thank you.

 SILHOUETTE BOOKS

ISBN 0-373-19408-0

THE BABY BENEATH THE MISTLETOE

Copyright © 1999 by Marie Rydzynski-Ferrarella

Visit us at www.romance.net

Printed in U.S.A.

Bundles of Joy

Dearest Reader,

One of my very favorite photographs of my daughter Jessi is when she was five months old. She's wearing her jammies and is sitting in her infant seat, right under the Christmas tree. She looks like a Christmas present. I thought of that photograph when I began writing this book. But with one change. Because *babies* are really more like something you'd want to find underneath your mistletoe—one look at their cute faces and you just want to cover them with kisses (at least I do). But like Christmas presents, you unwrap them, never knowing what you'll find.

In writing this story, I revisited the family I used in my first family saga for Silhouette Romance. The Marino-McClellan family is a little unconventional, because it features a married couple who already had one son but went on to adopt a foster brother and sister. They're like so many families these days. No longer are families just Mom, Dad, two and a half kids and a dog. What has resulted in all this is the understanding that, essentially, to be a family, all you really need is love. Once you have that, the rest is easy. At least, that's what my protagonists discover.

Here's wishing you love, now and always.

Love,

Marie Ferrarella

Chapter One

"She's driving me absolutely crazy," Tony Marino said.

Shad McClellan and Angelo Marino, two-thirds of Marino, McClellan & Conrad Construction Company, exchanged grins at their cousin's very vocal, very intense complaint. Tony, Angelo thought, finally had a little color in his face and more than a little emotion in his voice. It was about time and in his opinion, a very good sign.

Technically, Antonio Marino was only Angelo's cousin, at least in terms of blood. But on that long-ago day when Angelo's parents had thrown open their door and their hearts to two motherless children, Shad and his younger sister Dottie, Angelo had embraced both Shad and Dottie as his equals and his siblings in every sense of the word but legal. There were some things that transcended legalities and rules. Like love.

Heaven knew Tony could certainly use a little love

himself right now. Or maybe a lot, Angelo amended, given what Tony had been through in the last year.

"Driving you crazy, huh? I take it you don't mean that in a good way."

"Good way?" Tony echoed with an incredulous, dismissive snort. *That'll be the day.*

Trying to curb his temper, Tony ran a restless hand through the black mop of hair that stubbornly insisted on falling into his eyes, much the way it had when he was a boy. But that boy would never have thought his heart could have been so completely and painfully ripped out of his chest as it had been a little more than a year ago.

Lines about his mouth, mirroring the ones etched into his soul, deepened as he thought of the short, opinionated architect who could make herself heard above a hurricane. She had become, in an incredibly short period of time, the total bane of his existence. Tony didn't need to be saddled with this problem. It was all he could do to remember to put one foot in front of the other. To get through each day. Overseeing the construction project was hard enough without having to deal with her.

"*Good* and *Michelle Rozanski* do *not* belong in the same sentence." Tony rolled his own words over in his head. "Same sentence? Hell, they don't belong in the same zip code."

Wanting to show his cousins just what he was up against, Tony began rifling through the chaotic disorder on the tiny, scarred metal desk, looking for the blueprints that they were supposed to be using to build Bedford's newest high school.

Shad glanced at Angelo again. This was the most emotion any of the family had seen Tony display since they had first coerced him to leave Denver and stay with them in Bedford. His sister had been right. Throwing Tony headlong into a brand-new project for the company had been the right thing to do. Dottie had known that he needed to have his mind on something other than his pain.

"It can't be as bad as all that," Shad commented.

A lot he knew, Tony thought darkly. Neither he nor Angelo had had any more to do with the feisty pain in the butt than exchange a few words at the initial meeting at city hall. They certainly hadn't had to endure her incessant contradictions at every opportunity. *Bad* didn't come anywhere near explaining the day-to-day work environment. He'd thought his association with the architect would begin and end with that brief meeting at city hall to accept the blueprints. He hadn't realized the meeting would be only the beginning—the beginning of constant daily warfare in which his side appeared to be sustaining the most casualties. He never knew when she could come flying in through the trailer door with another bone to pick, another change to argue. He'd taken to locking it, just to claim a little peace of mind.

"It's worse," Tony snapped. Where the hell was that blueprint? The one of the second floor off the high school's music-and-arts complex. He'd just had it. Tony shoved more papers aside. "She has an opinion on everything."

"Most women do," Shad deadpanned, trying to hide his grin behind his hand. This was looking very promising. When Tony had first arrived on his aunt Bridgette Marino's doorstep a little over two months ago, he'd been a shell of the young man who had worked long summers beside them at one construction site after another. The light and laughter that had always been in his cousin's green eyes had completely vanished.

Now at least there was something there. Granted, anger wasn't the greatest emotion, but it was better than nothing. It meant he was coming alive again, beginning to react to things around him instead of just sleepwalking through each day.

Knocking over an oversize, red-bound book, Tony continued searching. "Not like this."

Frustrated, he glanced up at the other two men. "She thinks she's right—" Then Tony bit off a curse as another falling book narrowly missed his toe. He'd never been a very organized person, but in the past thirteen months he'd found himself facing nothing but chaos everywhere he turned. Which was just the way he felt inside.

"At the risk of repeating myself," Angelo said amiably. "Most women do."

Most women, but not Teri, Tony thought, the memory bringing with it the sharp, deep stab of pain. Teri, with her quiet, unassuming soul. So quiet and unassuming that at times he'd all but had to coax responses out of her. She'd always been more than willing to bow to his wishes, uncontested.

He supposed in a way that had spoiled him. It certainly hadn't prepared him to deal with a blue-eyed, sharp-tongued wrecking ball who was unshakably convinced that everything she said was etched in stone somewhere, residing on the same shelf as the Ten Commandments.

"Maybe," Tony said. "But not like this." Finding what he'd been searching for, shoved under the stained blotter, of all places, he pulled it out and made a futile attempt to smooth the long, curled paper out on top of his desk. "Have either of you taken a close look at these blueprints of hers?"

His patience in drastically short supply, Tony gave up trying to flatten out the paper on the cluttered surface and rounded his desk. Beckoning his cousins forward, Tony crouched down, placing the blueprint on the floor and spreading it out there.

Tony wasn't sure just where to begin. Aesthetically pleasing, the proposed complex for the high school had more than one trouble spot. Several sections of the buildings appeared to, for all intents and purposes, simply defy the laws of physics. He stabbed a finger at what appeared to be the worst offense. He singled out the king post beneath the glass section of the roof.

"There, look at that. The woman actually thinks that's possible."

Shad and Angelo looked and saw the inherent flaw. Tony was right, at least to some extent. It would take a little compromising on both parts to work around the problem. But both men felt that Tony was up to it, given time. Relative or not, no matter how much their hearts went out to him in his time of emotional turmoil, neither Shad nor Angelo would have handed him the assignment if they hadn't thought him equal to it. After all, he was a damned good civil engineer.

Since they had begun expanding their firm, merging with Conrad & Son when Angelo's wife, Allison, came aboard, they'd had more new business than Salvator Marino could ever have conceived of when he'd originally started the small company. Then the company had been restricted to remodeling and upgrading bathrooms. Now there were no such restrictions on their expertise. More than one of the newer shopping malls in Southern California bore the stamp of their labor.

Nodding his head as if he were commiserating with Tony, Angelo looked at the man beside him and said, "Handle it."

"I've been *trying* to handle it." Tony knew he wasn't the type to complain at the slightest provocation, but there was just something about this woman that seemed to set him off. Maybe it was how she looked at him—smug, determined, ready to cut him down to size. Or maybe it was just that he'd jumped in when he should have started out wading. Maybe this was too much of a project to take on, and he shouldn't have agreed to do it.

He was tired, he told himself. Too tired to be reasonable tonight. Maybe things would look better on Monday.

"If I try to handle it anymore," he said to his easy-going cousin, "my fingers will be wrapping around her throat." Unconsciously he rubbed his thumbs along his forefingers. He had to admit the thought had some merit to it.

Angelo laughed. "I said handle it, not her."

Tony's frown deepened. "Handling *it* means handling her."

Still squatting over the blueprints, Tony looked down at them again. Heading up an operation was nothing new to him. He'd been in charge of enough of them at his old company, and coming back to work for Marino, McClellan & Conrad was essentially like coming home again, at least for the most part. But he'd been at the top of his game before. Now he had trouble pulling his thoughts together for more than a few minutes at a time, trouble moving from the beginning of each day to the end of it.

It never seemed to get any better.

He'd returned to Bedford, to his roots, at the very insistent request of his aunt Bridgette. The rest of the family had been quick to throw in their support, each inviting him to stay with them. He'd agreed to come out because it had been an almost unconscious, last-ditch attempt on his part to leave the land of the walking wounded and reenter the land of the living.

Turning down their offers, he'd leased an apartment for himself and tried to make a new start.

But it wasn't working, not really. He didn't belong here any more than he had back in Denver, his home for the past eight years.

He didn't belong anywhere in this world, now that Teri and Justin weren't in it.

Hopelessness began to spread long, icy fingers over him again, reclaiming him for its own. Freezing everything inside him.

He didn't want to repay Angelo and Shad for their kindness by screwing up. It wasn't right.

Tony sat back on his heels, talking to both of them, looking at neither. "Maybe you'd be better off if I just bowed out of this." He sighed, feeling drained. "I have a feeling that I've bitten off more than I can chew." He was almost sure of it. He turned toward Angelo. "Maybe you—"

Angelo hated seeing him like this. Tony had always been equal to every challenge. But death had a way of changing all that. "Sorry, I've got the Carmichael project on my hands."

Tony looked to the other man. "Shad?"

Shad already had his hands up, warding off the request Tony was about to make. "I'm handling the Gaetti development over at the north end of the city."

Tony thought of the third member of the company.

Emotionally shut off, he hadn't really taken the time to get to know Angelo's wife, but he knew her name wouldn't be on the logo if she wasn't first class. Which was why *he* didn't belong here.

Raising a brow, he looked toward Angelo again. "Allison?"

Angelo shook his head. "Besides handling the triplets," he said, pride and respect evident in his voice, "she's working on that next phase of the Winwood homes south of here."

Tony had forgotten about that. If he'd been in form, he thought ruefully, he would have remembered. Remembered everything. Still...

"Is there anyone else you can give this to?"

"Sorry, buddy. Ma and Dottie don't do construction and Frankie's too busy taking classes at UCI in between fighting off girls," Angelo said, mentioning Shad's stepson. It had been a disappointment when he'd discovered that Frankie, though incredibly adept at the work, had absolutely no interest in joining the family firm when he finally graduated from college at the end of this spring. "So there's nobody left to helm this thing, but you. There's no time to go scouting around for a new member."

Shad clamped a hand on Tony's shoulder. "I'm afraid the family honor and reputation are both in your almost uncallused hands."

A very decisive knock on the trailer door tabled any further discussion among them. Shad felt Tony stiffen beneath his hand, a fatigued soldier suddenly going on the alert because he'd heard what he assumed was the approach of the enemy just outside his foxhole.

Tony wasn't kidding about the fireworks between them, Shad thought. But fireworks could be either de-

structive or celebratory, depending on the way circumstances arranged themselves. A little guidance was in
order here.

Being closest to the door, Angelo rose to his feet to
open it. The smile that came to his lips was automatic.
He had always appreciated beauty, whether in the lines
of a well-constructed edifice, the multi-hued rays of a
sunrise, or a striking woman. Which was now the case.

At five-one and barely a hundred pounds, Michelle
Rozanski lit up any space she occupied and, at least in
Angelo's opinion, looked like an unlikely candidate to
be a driven architect. In his experience most architects
were bespectacled, slightly hunched men who spent a
good deal of their time leaning over elongated desks
and squinting at tiny white lines inscribed on blue paper. The computer had only changed the angle at which
they squinted.

Mikky, as everyone called her, looked as if she
should have a beribboned, noisy tambourine in her
hand, a wide, colorful skirt swirling about her slim hips
and an ankle bracelet made of entwined, fresh-cut flow-
ers resting just above her bare feet. Despite the short,
elfinlike hairstyle she wore, the word *gypsy,* sprang instantly to his mind when he looked at her. *Architect*
didn't even remotely venture into the picture.

But she was a good one, if he were to believe her
reputation. Certainly good enough to catch the eye and
the fancy of most of the members of Bedford's city
council. It was Mikky's lofty design for the new fifteen-
acre high school that had won out over more than sev-
enty-five other bids from far more prestigious firms.

Of course, just because the design, with its five very
different buildings surrounding a gardenlike center, was
aesthetically appealing, it wasn't necessarily doable, he

thought. He'd learned that more than once. What Tony had just pointed out to them was evidence of that. But that was a bone he figured his cousin was just going to have to chew on himself. As far as Angelo was concerned, it would undoubtedly do Tony good.

He needed to feel his blood rushing in his veins again, not have it all but congeal there.

Mixed signals assaulted Mikky the moment she stepped into the trailer. From the partners of the company, she felt an aura of genial accord. That, she had to admit, was a fairly new sensation. Accustomed to having to wage what amounted, at times, to a fierce battle to win respect on every project she undertook, she was surprised and pleased at Angelo's and Shad's reactions to her. But then, she'd heard they were fair men who knew their stuff. It didn't hurt that the third member of their firm was a woman, either.

There was no question in Mikky's mind that Shad and Angelo were men she could certainly work with. There was no macho challenge in their eyes when they looked at her, or worse, a feeling that she was being undressed and dissected. Even in this day and age, it wasn't an uncommon thing for her to come up against this sort of sexual bias. And, though she had to admit that Tony Marino rankled her down to her very toes, at least he wasn't guilty of that sort of insulting behavior, either.

The insults, both implied and vocalized, took another form. Tony Marino was blatantly in contempt of her intelligence. To Mikky that was a far greater offense. She'd worked hard to get to where she was, struggled every inch of the way for her schooling and to acquire a position with a prestigious firm. Once she'd gotten there, she'd had no respite. Even in these supposedly enlightened times, there were those who thought she'd slept her way to her position.

It was butting up against that lie that had finally given her the courage to hand in her resignation to Finch, Crown & Ferguson, a company that had been around for nearly eighty years, and begin her own company. The fact that her rendition of the new high school had won out over so many others told her that she had made the right decision in sticking to her guns and to her dreams.

And no sexy-looking, hard-bodied, small-minded construction boss in form-fitting jeans was going to make her believe otherwise, she thought fiercely, her eyes shifting to him now.

If Tony Marino wanted to fight her every step of the way to get "her" building up, well then so be it. She was up to the war. Thrived on it, even. Mikky came from a large family where fighting was as much a part of the day as breakfast.

Shad shook Mikky's hand in greeting. "To what do we owe this honor?" Behind him, he heard Tony murmur something under his breath. Shad smiled to himself. Any reaction besides passive was a good one.

Mikky drew herself up to her full height, refusing to be intimidated by the fact that when Tony got to his feet, she was surrounded by three men who were almost a foot taller than she was. She felt her determination and talent made up the difference in physical stature.

"I came because I was summoned." Her eyes shifted to Tony. "What is it now, Marino? I hope this won't take long. I was getting ready to leave."

Tony shoved his hands into the back pockets of his jeans. "Permanently?"

He'd been trying to get rid of her from the first. "For the weekend."

"Pity."

"Make you a deal," she proposed. "You save your pity, and I'll save mine." She saw the blueprint spread out on the floor. Was he using it as a floor mat now? She wouldn't put it past him. "Now, what's your problem—other than the obvious?"

Tony squared his shoulders and grabbed the paper from the floor, all but holding it up before her nose. "Unless someone rewrote the laws of physics when I wasn't looking, you're still as wrong about this now as you were this morning when I brought it up."

There was enough electricity crackling in the room to keep an entire city lit up for a year, Shad thought. Catching Angelo's eye, he nodded ever so slightly. They were in agreement. Time to retreat. Shifting positions with Mikky, he backed up toward the door. Angelo was already there.

"Well, we'll leave you two to your negotiations," Shad said more to Mikky than to Tony.

Tony opened his mouth in protest, but never got the chance. Angelo was way ahead of him.

"We'll see you at dinner on Sunday." Rather than becoming a thing held only in childhood memories, dinner at his mother's house was a tradition that had strengthened as the years went by and as their numbers had doubled and continued to increase. "If you're free," Angelo couldn't resist saying to Mikky, "maybe you'd like to come, too. Ma always says there's room for one more at the table. Tony can give you the address. Can't you, Tony?"

Stunned at what he felt was an outright act of betrayal, Tony clamped his lips together. Why were his cousins bailing out on him this way, looking so smug about it? Didn't they see that the last thing he needed now was someone like Mikky Rozanski?

Some family they were.

Mikky waited until Angelo and Shad had left and the door to the trailer was closed before turning toward Tony again.

The invitation from the man's cousins had made her feel warm. In contrast, any exchange with Tony just made her feel hot. Hot under the collar and braced to go the full fifteen rounds of a championship fight in which she had to be the winner in order to survive in this field. She couldn't afford to look as if she didn't know what she was doing. Word spread too fast in the architectural community, and although the number of female architects was growing, there were still not enough to make her feel comfortable and at ease. Sometimes she felt as if she were carrying the standard for all women in the male-dominated field.

God, but the man did look formidable when he was annoyed, she thought, her eyes quickly sweeping over him. She couldn't help wondering what his face looked like when it was relaxed, or when he was laughing. She had yet to see him even attempt a smile. Something told her that it would not be an unpleasant sight, but she doubted if she'd ever get to witness it firsthand.

It didn't matter. She wasn't here to make friends, just a good reputation.

Vowing to keep her own temper in check no matter what, she looked at Tony expectantly. She wanted to get this over with as quickly as possible because she didn't want to be late for the movie she'd promised to catch with her brother, Johnny. "Well?"

Tony didn't like her tone. She'd walked in on a meeting he'd had earlier with Mendoza, the foreman, taking him to task for changes she'd discovered he was about to make on her design. She'd had the nerve to all but order him to take another look before he struck out so much as a single line.

He'd been on the phone most of the morning, tracking down a shipment of conduit wiring that had mysteriously gone astray and hadn't had time to go over their newest bone of contention at length. But he didn't feel he had to. Right was right, no matter how thoroughly it was examined.

"'Well' nothing, you know what I have to say."

He folded the blueprints back so that the design was showing on both sides and indicated the area they were coming at from opposite ends. How could she not see how obvious the problem was?

Talking as if he were explaining it to a slow-witted child, he said, "You can't have the mezzanine sticking out this far. It jeopardizes the integrity of the floor joist here, not to mention the ridge beam." Stopping, he began to deliberately point out the long, straight lines below the roof. "That's this—"

Mikky curbed the urge to swat his hand away from the blueprints. "I *know* where the ridge beam is." Mikky had no doubt that if she were a man, Marino wouldn't have been talking down to her that way.

"Fine. Then you also know that if you eliminate the mezzanine—"

"I am *not* going to eliminate the mezzanine." The man was nothing short of a shark, she thought, her temperature rising despite all her promises to herself. With unerring instinct, he was going for an area vital to her style. Mikky had worked hard to incorporate that into her design. The music-and-arts complex was the jewel in the five-building setting.

Blowing out an angry breath, he looked at her. "What do high school students need with a mezzanine?"

Now he was talking nonsense. "What does anyone need with pleasing shapes and sleek lines? Why five buildings? Why not just make everything into a great big ugly box?" Realizing her voice had gone up, Mikky stopped using hand gestures to underscore her words and attempted to rein in her irritation. "Because it's more aesthetic this way, that's why."

Tony had no idea why, when she mentioned pleasing shapes and sleek lines, his eyes had been drawn to Mikky's own form. They were talking—arguing—about a building. A building that wasn't going to go up if it had to be according to her design.

There was absolutely no reason for him to notice that when her voice went up an octave, her breasts strained against the plum-colored sweater she was wearing. Who the hell wore colors like that to a construction site, anyway? he thought in irritation. "Aesthetic?" He spat out the word. "They're there to learn, not philosophize." He believed in solid, utilitarian construction, not gingerbread and sugar that melted in the first rain. And this kind of design was wasted on the audience it was to have. "Kids that age haven't got enough in their heads to philosophize about, anyway. All they think about is having fun, nothing else."

Memories clawing at him, Tony turned away to collect himself. Everything kept going back to that, to the moment his life had been irrevocably shattered.

Mikky watched his back, saw the silent struggle being waged, saw the tension in his shoulders. She knew his story. Had asked around after their first meeting. He'd struck her as a walking ice palace, and she'd wanted to know why. She'd had one of her brothers, an investigative reporter on the staff of the *L.A. Times,* nose around for her. Johnny had come across a story in the *Denver Post.* Marino's wife and three-year-old son had been killed in a car crash, both dying instantly when a teenage driver, drunk and out joyriding with his friends, had slammed into their car. Marino had been away at an engineering conference at the time.

Sympathy was something that came as naturally to Mikky as breathing. Even sympathy for someone who kept biting her head off. She figured he had issues to work out. But she wouldn't have him do it at her expense.

Her voice softened. "Look, I'm sorry about your wife and little boy—"

His head snapping up, Tony looked at her sharply, his eyes dark and dangerous. She'd jabbed a long, narrow pin deep inside an open wound. She had no business even approaching it.

"Thanks." The word was covered with so much frost, Mikky thought she was in danger of losing all feeling in her extremities. "But I'd appreciate if you didn't mention them. This has nothing to do with them." He looked at the blueprint. "These are teenagers. They're supposed to be attending school to learn. All they need are classrooms, not mezzanines or enclosed atriums or cascading waterfalls—"

She was trying to be understanding, but he was pushing her to the limit. This was her work he was criticizing so cavalierly. Like a mother coming to her child's defense, Mikky felt her adrenaline beginning to rise. The whole point of the design was to come up with something that was in keeping with the larger scheme of things within the city. Bedford was on record as a planned community—a place where everything was a celebration of shapes and colors, that strove also for balance and harmony within the community. Was he determined to ruin that just for the sake of argument?

The Southwood High complex was going to be the first building block to forge her reputation and as such was of tantamount importance to her. This was her first solo baby, and she meant to do right by it. And have it do right by her.

Maybe that made her a tad overprotective of the design. But she'd made absolutely certain she'd been right in her calculations—that there were no faults, no surprises—and she was going to stick to her guns come hell or high water.

Or a man named Tony Marino.

"Then, why don't we just build a little red schoolhouse and be done with it?" she challenged.

"Don't get sarcastic with me."

Far from being intimidated, Mikky fisted her hands on her hips, anger bubbling inside of her at a breathtaking speed. Its very advent took her by surprise. While no one had ever accused her of being easygoing, she'd never been one to overheat quickly, either. But there was something about Marino that lit her fuse. "Then don't get belligerent with me. I'm just trying to do a job, same as you."

The hell she was. There was nothing the same about them, and there never would be. Tony felt as if the trailer had somehow grown even more cramped than it already was. "No, what you are trying to do is challenge everything I say."

He made it sound as if Mikky enjoyed beating her

head against his stone wall. Maybe that was Marino's idea of a good time, but it certainly wasn't hers. "When you're wrong—"

He slapped the blueprint down on his desk, underlining his point. "There, you just did it again."

Mikky opened her mouth, then clamped it shut again. This wasn't getting them anywhere. This was going to escalate until they were both shouting at each other, and she didn't want to wind up saying things she couldn't take back.

She held up her hands, not in surrender but in a gesture calculated to make him back off. "Okay, why don't we go back to our corners and wait for the bell to sound on a new round?"

Tony didn't have patience with analogies. On the outskirts of his mind it occurred to him that he didn't have much patience with anything lately. She just seemed to bring it out more radically.

"Meaning?"

Trying not to grit her teeth together, Mikky spelled it out for him. "Meaning, why don't you—why don't we," she amended, knowing that to leave the suggestion in the singular was asking for trouble, "take the weekend to cool off and start again—fresh—Monday morning?" She figured that was only fair. Given the hour, he couldn't take exception with that. "I'll think about what you said and you—" picking up the blueprint from his desk, Mikky took out her pen and drew a few lines beneath the offending mezzanine on the upper right-hand corner "—think about this."

What she had drawn in, in her estimation, should do the trick to offset the stress problem he had pointed out to her. Though she hated to admit it, it had been an oversight on her part. An oversight that any normal construction manager would have realized and remedied easily, without any dramatic denouncements and billows of fire coming out of his nostrils every time he spoke to her.

"There." She thrust the paper back at him, then went to the door. "I'll see you Monday. And don't worry, nice though it would be to meet the saner members of your family, I have no intention of taking Angelo up on his invitation for Sunday dinner at your aunt's house." Mikky pulled open the door, more than ready to leave all this behind her for the space of two days. "I have trouble swallowing when daggers are being flung at me."

The door closed behind her with a resounding slam before Tony had a chance to say anything.

He stared at the blueprint. Muttering a curse that was aimed at him rather than her, he crumpled the paper between his hands and tossed it aside. She was right, damn her. About more than one thing. Which annoyed him even more.

But annoyed or not, it didn't negate the fact that he was acting like a jerk, he thought reproachfully. He just couldn't help himself. He was trying to get on with his life, he really was, but he kept tripping over his own feet while looking for the right path.

There didn't seem to be one.

He knew they meant well—Angelo, Shad and the others. Maybe even that aggravating woman who had just sauntered out of here swinging those sleek, tight hips of hers meant well, though he doubted it. But all the good intentions in the world weren't working.

Moving around to the other side of his desk, he yanked open the bottom drawer and took out the half-pint of whisky he'd purchased. He'd brought it with him on the first day, leaving it in the drawer for when he needed it. Hoping he wouldn't. But he felt as if he'd reached the end of the line right now. Coming here had been his last hope, and things were just not coming together. Instead, they felt as if they were unraveling. He was losing his temper more frequently, ready to fly off the handle over things he should have been able to take in stride. His life was spinning out of control, and there was nothing he could do to stop it. But at least he could anesthetize himself to it for a while.

Taking the bottle out, he held it in his hand, staring at the amber liquid. He had to get away, go off somewhere by himself and work this out. He'd been wrong to come here, wrong to put everyone through this with him.

Unscrewing the cap, he brought the top to his lips. It wasn't their problem, it was—

The slight rap on the door made him freeze. Thinking maybe he'd imagined it, Tony listened closely. He heard it again. Though it was completely different from her earlier knock, he immediately thought of Mikky. The woman had probably decided to have another go at him despite all her talk about their taking a breather. Obviously the scent of blood drew her in, just like a scavenger.

Capping the bottle, he put the untouched half-pint back in the drawer and closed it. He knew he should apologize to Mikky for the way he lost his temper, but he wasn't feeling very apologetic as he crossed to the door.

With a yank, Tony pulled it open. "Look, if you want to continue this fight, then—"

His words had no audience. Mikky wasn't standing on his doorstep. No one was. Leaning out, he looked around, but he didn't see anyone. Darkness blanketed everything.

And then a gurgling sound caught his ear. A gurgling sound coming from just about his shoe level. Puzzled, he looked down.

It was then that he saw the baby.

Chapter Two

Why do you let him get to you like that? Annoyed with herself, Mikky locked the door of the small trailer that housed her drawing board and all the miscellaneous paraphernalia she'd brought with her. Absently she slipped the key ring onto her finger and then, pulling her jacket closer, she strode toward where she'd left her car parked.

In the distance she saw the lone security guard looking her way. She waved. The German shepherd he kept with him barked once, acknowledging her movement in something less than friendly tones. Mikky dropped her hand.

It wasn't as if she wasn't versed in verbal combat. She was and she was damn good at it. Hadn't she grown up with four brothers and three sisters? Didn't she know how to hold her own, even when it was against more than one of them at a time? And wasn't she the one who always struck a blow for common sense and common ground?

Because it was cold, even for a Southern California December, she shoved her hands into her pockets as she hurried along. All right, maybe not every time, she amended, but enough times to really count.

So why did she feel as if a match was being struck to her every time she found herself talking to that—to that pompous, foul-tempered—

Mikky let the thought go, knowing that pasting a label on Marino would only make things worse in her mind. She wasn't here to fight, she was here to do a job, to see her project through to its completion. This was the first big contract she'd won on her own. Name calling wasn't going to help her along toward her goal.

Even if it did feel good.

Arriving at her car, she unlocked the door and tossed her purse in on the passenger side before sliding in herself. Much as she hated the thought, what she did need to do was apologize to the big ape and do her best to seem congenial and sincere about it.

She started her car as she rolled the thought over in her mind.

Maybe if she got him to relax, she could handle him.

Yeah, right. Fat chance of that happening. The man could only be handled by an experienced lion tamer with a tranquilizer gun. Sighing, she began the slow, bumpy drive through the site, heading for the street in the distance.

Still, she didn't want to take a chance on coming away with a bad reputation. All she wanted to do was get her damn design up—as close to its original conception as possible.

It wasn't that she was being stubborn. She wasn't so stubborn that she couldn't be shown the error of her thinking—if there was an error—but it had to be done in a civilized fashion. She refused to be barked at.

Belatedly, she turned on her lights. Bright yellow beams cut through the encroaching dusk. Her father had always barked at her, she remembered. His grousing had made her reexamine her every move. Years later she'd discovered that, despite his outwardly gruff manner, her father had been that way with her to make her strong. In his own fashion he'd tried to prepare her for the world. Walter Rozanski firmly believed that life was there to bring a person to his knees, and he wanted none of his children to be forced into that position. Riding them was the only way he knew how to make them fit enough to meet the hardships along the way.

Maybe Marino reminded her of her father, Mikky thought with a sudden shiver. Or maybe he just reminded her of a bad-tempered bear. In any event it was up to her to get along with the man. Once this job was completed, if the fates were kind, she would never have to interact with Tony Marino again.

Mikky paused, hesitating just before she drove off the lot. She looked toward Marino's trailer. The light was still on. Except for his car, and the guard's beat-up truck, the lot was empty. Everyone else had gone home for the weekend. There would be no one to come in and interrupt her if she apologized to him.

Vacillating for a few moments, Mikky took a deep, cleansing breath and blew it out, then made her decision. Okay, it was now or never, before she thought better of this madness and changed her mind.

The things a person had to do for the sake of peace, she thought grudgingly. She wasn't naive enough to think that any sort of real harmony could come out of this, but it would be nice if the sniping would stop.

Mikky guided her car along the uneven, freshly graded dirt toward the trailer. Reaching it, she pulled up the hand brake, put the car into Park and turned the engine off.

Nothing rankled her more than apologizing when she didn't feel as if she was in the wrong. But she wasn't selling out, she told herself as she got out. She was doing this so she could get on with the work. So her name could be associated with this brand-new high school, and hopefully with a lot of other new projects and developments as yet unplanned.

It wasn't selling out, it was having good business sense.

The silent pep talk didn't help. Walking up the three steps to his trailer, she knocked on the door. There was no immediate answer, and she almost left before forcing herself to knock again.

This time she thought she heard a cat mewling inside the trailer. Odd, she didn't remember seeing a cat, and she was certain someone would have mentioned it to her if Marino kept a cat on the premises.

Actually, now that she listened, she thought the noise sounded more like—

"A baby."

The incredulous words tumbled from her lips as Tony opened the door. In the crook of one arm, held awkwardly against his chest, was a baby. She judged it to be approximately nine months old. It was wrapped up in a faded, torn, blue blanket.

Stunned, Mikky raised her eyes to his. "What are you doing with a baby?"

Great, Tony thought, this was all he needed to add to the confusion he was already wading through. He leaned out again to see if there was someone lurking in the shadows, ready to capitalize on this practical joke they were playing. But the lot was as empty now as it had been five long minutes ago.

The sinking sensation that this was no joke was beginning to penetrate.

"Holding it." Tony ground out the words.

"Besides that?" Mikky asked, shouldering her way past him into the trailer. As she moved by him, she took the baby into her own arms.

Though a protest initially leaped to his lips, Tony surrendered his burden willingly. One glance at Mikky forced him to admit that she had a far better feel for holding a child that size than he did. It had been a long time since he'd held a baby in his arms. The bittersweet memories holding it evoked was just about doing him in.

He didn't need this on top of everything else.

Mikky knew for a fact that Marino had no other children. What was he doing with this baby? Turning to look at him, she saw that there was no explanation forthcoming. It figured.

"Well?" Opening her jacket, she cradled the baby against her, enjoying the warm feel of its small, rounded body. Maternal feelings that had long been sublimated leaped up within her. She wanted children. A whole house full of them. Unable to resist, she kissed the small head. "Where did it come from?"

His wide shoulders rose and fell. "I found it on the doorstep."

Why did every scrap of information she got from him first have to be preceded by a tug-of-war? "No, I mean really."

"Really," he insisted. Tony gestured toward a beaten-up baby seat. "The baby was in that."

Cooing soothing noises at the small invader, Mikky turned to look at the baby seat. It looked as if it had been in service a very long time. The baby was making sucking sounds against her shoulder that she recognized as hunger in the making. It was going to need baby food and milk and soon.

With one hand holding the child in place, she picked up the blanket from the baby seat and shook it. A creased envelope fell out.

Unable to open it herself, Mikky held the envelope out to Tony. She couldn't help wondering if her initial sympathy for him was misguided. Maybe there was more to this man than she'd thought. Maybe this was his baby....

"Want to read it?"

Tony took the envelope from her before the tone of her voice registered. He looked at her sharply. "Why? You think it's mine?"

"Is it?"

His laugh was short and completely devoid of humor. "Only in a parallel universe."

He hadn't looked at another woman since he'd met Teri, much less engaged in a liaison with one. And there had been no one since his wife's death. He was completely dead inside.

Annoyed at her, he tore open the envelope, taking off a corner of the note with it. Ignoring Mikky, he shook the note out and quickly read it. There wasn't much to read.

Curious, unable to see anything in his expression, Mikky stood on her toes to look around his arm at the note herself.

"Please take care of Justin. I know you can," she

read out loud. No help there. She looked at Tony. "Not much to go on, is it?"

Instead of answering right away, Tony dropped the note on his desk, letting it land on the blueprint, which, she noticed, looked far more crumpled now than when she'd left a few minutes earlier. That it was apparently smoothed out again indicated he'd obviously had a change of heart about his feelings. He was a hard man to figure out, she thought.

"No," Tony answered, his voice very still, "it's not." He felt as if someone had just dropped an anvil on his chest.

Moving into the light so she could get a better look at his face, Mikky saw that his olive complexion had grown almost pale. "What's the matter?"

His eyes averted, Marino refused to even look at her. "Nothing."

Mikky was tired of having him bite the hand she kept offering in friendship. She took the same tone she took with one of her brothers on the infrequent occasions when their moods turned nasty.

"Don't 'nothing' me." When he began to turn from her, she butted her hand against his shoulder and pushed him back around so that he was forced to face her. He looked at her in mute surprise. "I was raised in a house full of brothers, and I know when a man's trying to hide something. Now what's wrong? You turned pale when you said the baby's name."

She was going to harp on this until he caved, Tony thought angrily. It was none of her damn business, but he told her anyway. "Justin was my son's name."

"Oh." Where did she go from here, hobbling the way she was with her foot in her mouth? Mikky thought. She caught her lower lip in her teeth. "I'm sorry."

His scowl grew darker. "I don't need you to be sorry."

The war was on again. It figured. His type didn't know how to show any emotion other than growling. "Okay," she said tersely. "Moving on. Did you see anyone?" The baby was beginning to leave a very wet spot on her shoulder where he was sucking on her blouse.

Tony shook his head, frustrated. Why had someone singled him out? There had to be a reason, didn't there? What was it?

"There was a knock on the door. I thought maybe it was you, coming back to apologize. When I opened the door, there wasn't anyone there, except for him." He nodded toward the baby.

It was exactly what she was coming back to do— apologize—but his thinking she had reason to suddenly threw a fresh log onto the dying fire of Mikky's anger.

Her eyes widened as she looked at him. "Why should I apologize?"

"Because—"

But before he could continue, she held up a hand, waving away whatever it was he was going to say that would undoubtedly launch them into another round.

"Never mind, forget I asked. That isn't important now." She moved the baby into the crook of her arm. The smile that was on the rosebud mouth threatened to completely melt her heart. "But this baby is. What are you going to do about him?"

"Me? You're the one who's holding him. Possession is nine-tenths of the law, remember?"

There had to be more to this. Some kind of connection he wasn't admitting to.

"Whoever left him on your doorstep," she pointed out, "obviously thought you could take care of him." She consciously avoided using the baby's name, though she thought of it as an odd coincidence.

Take care of a baby? Tony thought. That was laughable. He could barely take care of himself right now, much less anyone so helpless. It was all he could do to function in the morning.

He wasn't answering her, she thought. Was he just ignoring her, or didn't he know? Mikky tried again. "So what are you going to do?"

Tiny fists opened and closed, catching air. Tony watched despite his effort not to. "I have no idea."

Chapter Three

Confronted with his indecision, Mikky gave the situation only a moment's thought and passed the baby to Tony. One of her brothers was a police detective. He'd take it from here. "Well, the right thing to do is to turn him over to the police."

Without realizing it, Tony held the baby closer to him. The whimper told him he was holding Justin too tight. "For what, loitering?"

"If you'd stop being antagonistic toward me for a minute, you'd realize that—"

"I'm not turning him over to the police."

Why was he being so vehement about it? A minute ago he'd been ambivalent. The answer had to be because she'd been the one to make the recommendation. "They won't put him in a lineup. He'll go to social services and—"

The very word nudged forward memories. He remembered listening with disbelief as Shad had described what life had been like for him and Dottie after their parents had died. Tony could remember how grateful he'd felt, knowing he had two parents who loved him and were always there for him.

"And what…be shunted around from place to place until someone gives him a home? *If* they give him a home?" He thought of how he would have felt if this were *his* Justin facing these alternatives. There was no way he would allow something like that to happen to the boy.

She had no idea why she was trying to talk sense into him. The man had a head like a rock. She doubted even a state of the art explosive could made a dent in it. "He's a foundling—"

"Yes, and I found him." He looked down at the small, round face. Several teeth underscored a half grin. Tony realized that he was already lost. "As you said, whoever left him thought I could take care of him." New resolve filled him. This wasn't about him right now. This was about a small, helpless human being. "And I'm going to."

He didn't know what he was letting himself in for. And Mikky didn't know why she didn't just say goodbye and go. Or why she should care what he did one way or the other. Maybe because she'd always been a sucker for the underdog, she thought. Even if the underdog insisted on snapping at her every word.

"Very noble." She nodded at the baby. "You could start by keeping his head up a little better."

Frowning, Tony realized that he'd let his hand slip. That was because she got him so irritated, he couldn't think straight. It was like hearing nails being run along a chalkboard. He was the board, she was the nails.

"I know," he snapped, moving his hand up. "I'm not a complete idiot."

"No, not a complete one," she allowed. "More like an idiot under construction."

"Look—"

"No, you look. The longer you hang on to the baby, the more attached you're going to get." And she could tell by the look in his eyes, he was halfway gone as it was. The little boy was nothing short of adorable.

What did it matter to her what he did? Tony wondered. And why did he feel called upon to justify himself to her? He owed her no explanations. And he'd given her more than the measure of courtesy she deserved.

"I'm just looking to doing the right thing," he heard himself saying.

"And the right thing is to turn the baby over to the police. They get cases like this all the time."

Tony snorted. "So they won't miss one if I don't hand him over to them. Look, the mother may have a change of heart—"

The dark, somber look that slipped over Mikky's fair features made Tony stop talking. "If she gave it up, she didn't have a heart—"

He was too tired to go around about this, or even wonder why her expression had hardened the way it did. "Why did you come back here, anyway?"

Irritated at Tony's lack of understanding, at his total pigheadedness, Mikky shouted her answer at him, momentarily forgetting that this had been his initial guess. "To apologize."

"Fine." His tone matched hers as he snapped back. "Apology accepted, now get out."

Turning on her heel, she stormed to the door. But then she stopped. Mikky blew out a breath and silently upbraided herself. She couldn't just leave him if he was determined to take the baby in.

With renewed determination to hang on to her temper, she turned around again. "We certainly rub each other the wrong way, don't we?"

Tony didn't even bother looking in her direction. His attention was focused on the baby, who had begun fussing at the sound of their raised voices. "Well, at least we agree on one thing."

She took a tentative step back toward him. "Why do you think that is?"

"Because for once you're right."

"No." Mikky tried not to lose her temper. "I meant about rubbing each other the wrong way."

Now she wanted to analyze things? Tony put no faith in that kind of nonsense, even if Dottie was a psychologist. Just a lot of words flying around as far as he was concerned. And he wanted none of them flying his way. "They include psych 101 in with your architect courses?"

"Just trying to find a way to get us to work better together."

Coming closer, Mikky leaned against his arm as she looked at the baby. She made a teasing face at Justin and was rewarded with a gurgle that was very close to a laugh. The sound went right through her, settling in her heart. He really was adorable, she mused.

The unintended brush of her breast against his arm evoked memories and aroused responses that were best left shut away. "You could start by butting out of my private life."

She raised her eyes to his. "*Is* this your baby?"

Why was she playing that same refrain over again?

He'd already told her once that it wasn't. That should have been enough. "Just for the time being."

She should go, Mikky thought. Get in her car and drive home. There was a weekend waiting for her and friends she could be getting together with if she wanted. And a brother to meet by a movie theater.

But she remained where she was, held fast by a conscience that had never learned how to sleep.

Very gently she pulled the edge of his sweater out of Justin's mouth. The baby seemed determined to eat whatever was handy. "You know anything about babies?"

"I know they don't have to be in inane conversations if they don't want to be." He moved, murmuring something to the baby, turning so that his back was to her.

She moved right along with him. "Neither do grouchy, stubborn men."

"If we, if *I*," he corrected, "turn Justin over to the police, the mother, *when* she comes back," he emphasized, unable to believe that any woman would willingly abandon a baby this way, "will be treated like a felon."

"There's a reason for that. Leaving your baby in a construction site *is* a felony. It's called abandonment."

He tried to think of the men who worked for him. The names and faces were still jumbled in his mind. He hadn't made a real effort to keep them straight. Did Justin belong to one of them?

Who could have been desperate enough to turn his back on a baby?

"Sometimes things aren't always cut-and-dried," he said, more to the baby than to her. "Sometimes they're confused."

Soft brown eyes turned to look up at Mikky as Justin turned his head in her direction. She could feel herself being drawn in. Feel herself growing angry at a woman she didn't know. "That doesn't mean you jettison a baby out of your life like extra baggage," she said, barely suppressing her anger.

"What makes you so hot under the collar about this? Justin wasn't left on your doorstep."

No, Mikky thought, he wasn't. And Tony hadn't had his mother walk out on him when he was a boy, leaving him to care for a squadron of brothers and sisters while nursing a broken heart. Her mother had left, no explanations, no excuses. She'd just taken a single suitcase of clothes and disappeared one day. And scarred an entire family with her departure.

Growing up fast hadn't been an option for her, it had been a necessity. Her older brother had falsified his birth certificate and enlisted in the Marines at seventeen. Her older sister had run off to get married at eighteen. She'd been left to look after the five younger ones.

Mikky shrugged carelessly. "I just don't like to see babies given a bad break, that's all."

There was something more to it, but Tony didn't feel like delving into it. Unlike Mikky, he respected boundaries.

He shifted the baby in his arms, nuzzling his neck. The sweet scent of sweat and powder nudged other memories to the fore, galvanizing his resolve.

"That's why I'm going to keep him with me."

She laughed shortly, shaking her head. "Like I said, I don't like seeing babies given a bad break."

If she wasn't going to leave, he was. He placed Justin back into the baby seat and began to redo the straps. They were worn and shredding in places. "I don't know why I'm even talking to you about this."

With a quiet sigh, Mikky moved him out of the way

and proceeded to tighten the straps herself. "Because you need help, and you don't know how to ask."

The way she just came in and elbowed him out of the way galled him no end. Just what gave her the right to think she could take over like this? "If I needed help, I wouldn't ask you for it."

"I know." Finished, she smiled at him. "Lucky for you I can read between the lines."

What the hell was she talking about now? "Lady, there *are* no lines."

"What do you feed a baby?"

The question, when he'd been expecting more barbs, caught him off guard. His mind went blank. "Stuff. Food. Milk."

He was just picking things out of the air, Mikky thought. Left alone long enough, even monkeys eventually typed out the encyclopedia. "Would you like to go on to iron filings?" she asked sweetly. Mikky lowered her face next to the baby. "See, he doesn't know the first thing about feeding you."

Straightening, she made up her mind, knowing she was probably going to regret this. "All right, you've talked me into it."

Like a man in a cartoon, Tony felt like looking behind him to see if there was someone else there. Someone else with whom she was carrying on a conversation. Because it certainly wasn't him. "Talked you into what?"

She pushed the strap of her purse up on her shoulder. "Helping you."

"When did I say that?"

The smile on her lips had to be upgraded just to be called patronizing, he thought darkly. "You didn't have to, the look your face says it all."

"If it did, we wouldn't be having this conversation—Not that it's much of a conversation, more like a monologue, and I just seem to be feeding you your cues."

It was getting late. If she worked this right, there still might be time to take in the last show with Johnny. She knew her brother wasn't going to be happy about that, but it couldn't be helped. "Let's get going before I change my mind."

Did she think that was a threat? Tony wondered. Okay, maybe he wasn't up on baby care, but how hard could it really be? "Oh, like it doesn't rotate 365 times every minute."

Stopped at the door, she raised her eyes to his. "If you're going to insult me—"

He had to stop short to keep from walking into her. At this proximity, looking down into her eyes, he found that they were an extremely dark shade of blue. It seemed as if nothing about her was in half measures. "Yes?"

Mikky thought of telling him off, of saying something curt in response, but where would that lead? Better that one of them kept their sense of humor, and since she seemed to be the only one who had one, it was up to her.

"Never mind, let's just go." Holding the door open, she waited until he stepped through with Justin. "There's a supermarket not too far from here. We should be able to get what we need there. At least for tonight. I'll lead, you follow."

He went down the steps, his eyes on the baby he was carrying. "What do you do when you're not being a drill sergeant?"

"I work on compiling a directory of polite men,"

she deadpanned. "So far, I'm not having any luck finding any." He was parked on the other side of the lot. She wondered if he was actually going to wait for her to pull her car around.

The night air was cold and the lot had an aura of isolation about it, even though Tony could see the headlights from passing cars just down the road. They were moving like tiny white jewels rolling down the road. "That's because they probably all hide when they see you coming."

She stopped at his car. Without waiting to be asked, she took Justin, baby seat and all, from him and let him fish out his car keys unencumbered. "Enough foreplay. We'll go shopping for a few essentials and then go to your place."

"My place?" He hadn't thought of her coming over. He hadn't thought that far ahead. This was getting way out of hand. "Be still my heart."

With the car door open, she handed Justin back to him. The next moment she was already sprinting back to her car. "To have your heart be still," she called out over her shoulder, "you would have had to have one beating in the first place."

He watched her go for a second, a moth watching the flame that was destined to kill it gain breadth and depth. "Touché," Tony murmured, fastening the baby seat in the rear passenger position. He always believed in giving the devil her due.

Shopping with Mikky, Tony quickly discovered, was not unlike trying to find evidence of footprints in a snowstorm. Just when he thought he saw her going down one aisle, she'd be heading for another. He had half a mind to leave without her, but in his heart he knew that she probably did have more experience at this than he did. The female of the species, he grudgingly allowed, had a better feel for this kind of thing. Even wolverines.

They went through the supermarket in record time, heading, by his watch, to the checkout line ten minutes after they'd entered the store. Feeling almost winded, Tony managed to finally catch up to her as she began to unload the basket.

Supermarkets weren't exactly his area of expertise. Since his world had been turned upside down, he'd done all of his food shopping at local convenience stores, dining on pop tarts, cereal that somehow managed to be perpetually stale no matter when he purchased it, and popcorn. If he wanted real food, there was always a fast-food restaurant around the corner to accommodate him.

"Do they give you discounts if you make it to the checkout line with a full basket in under fifteen minutes?" Before she could answer, he looked down at what she'd gathered. "What *is* all that?"

With an eye out for speed, Mikky grouped the goods together on the conveyor belt.

"Basics." She judged the baby to be under a year, but just barely. That meant he was into solids as long as it came in tiny jars. "You're going to need food, diapers, wipes, lotion, et cetera." To illustrate the latter, she held up a plastic toy that she'd grabbed on her way down aisle 12. It was a rabbit with an exaggerated, bewildered look on his face.

Somehow, the expression seemed rather appropriate, Tony mused. But he had his doubts about the rest of her booty. There seemed to be enough here to feed Justin until he went off to college. "All this?"

"All this," Mikky assured him. The baby was going to need clothes, she thought. Even if only a change or two over the weekend. She assumed that by Monday, Tony would either come to his senses, or the mother he seemed to have so much faith in would rethink her actions and return, looking for Justin.

She was hoping for the former, but wasn't taking any bets on either.

"Look, I'm not a novice at all this. But I don't remember having to get all this stuff."

"That's probably because your wife did the shopping." She pushed the cart ahead of her as their turn came. "You got to do the good stuff—the holding and the cuddling without the cleaning up." She cocked her head, looking at him. "Am I right?"

When he didn't answer her, she knew she was

But when she turned to look at him, the expression on his face made Mikky realize she'd inadvertently brushed up against something she'd had no intention of touching.

"I'm sorry." She lowered her voice so that only he could hear her clearly, "I didn't mean to jostle any memories."

He didn't answer. Instead Tony moved Mikky aside and took out his wallet. It vaguely occurred to him that it had been a while since he'd been to the bank. Glancing at the bills he took out of his wallet, he handed them to the cashier.

The checker took the money, counted it and then looked at him somewhat sheepishly. "You're short, sir."

Mikky realized that Tony had given the woman all he had in his wallet. "Actually, he's very tall for his age," she quipped, shifting attention to herself and covering for him. He'd undoubtedly be embarrassed to admit he was out of cash. "He's only ten. How much more do you need?"

The cashier glanced at the register, then down at her hand. "Three-fifteen."

Elbowing a stunned Tony out of the way, Mikky gave the woman four singles, then collected her change.

"What the hell was all that about?" he asked, sounding annoyed as they walked away from the checkout counter.

"Humor." Mikky pushed the cart through the electronic doors. "I was trying to lighten the situation all around." She raised her eyes to look at him. His expression was as somber as ever. "Obviously I failed with you." She stopped. "Switch places with me."

"What?"

"Switch places," she repeated, indicating the cart. "You push." Mikky nodded toward the baby. "I carry."

"Don't you trust me to carry the baby?"

Mikky began walking toward where they had parked their cars. She'd found a spot right beside his. "Just want to get in my fair share of time." It had been a long time since she'd held a baby in her arms, and she had to admit she'd missed the warm feeling that created.

An elderly woman walked by, pushing a moderately filled cart to her car. Entranced by Justin, she stopped to coo at him.

"She's adorable." The woman beamed at Mikky.

"He," Tony corrected. Opening up the trunk of his automobile, he began taking the groceries out of the cart and depositing them into the car.

The woman took her error in stride. "My mistake. Hard to tell these days." With the license that her advanced years gave her, she looked from Mikky to Tony. "How long have you two been married?"

"Just going on to two years," Mikky answered before Tony could set the woman straight. She saw the woman look at her in surprise as she unlocked her car. It was obvious she thought it unusual that they had come to the store in two separate vehicles. Mikky inclined her head toward the woman and said in a stage whisper, "That's the secret to a happy marriage. Separate cars."

The woman shuffled off, shaking her head.

Mikky laughed softly under her breath. When she turned around, she saw Tony looking at her. It was obvious that he hadn't a clue as to what made her tick and he knew it.

"You're certifiable, you know that?"

"If you're trying to flatter me, you need to brush up on your technique," she said.

He put the last of the groceries into his car and then closed the trunk. "And what's all this garbage about being married?"

Mikky lifted a shoulder carelessly and let it drop. She was beginning to enjoy riding him. This was far preferable to butting heads over designs and engineering points. "The woman was cooing over the baby. You didn't want her to think we were living together in sin, did you?"

"We're not living together at all." Tony caught himself before his voice went up, then stopped and looked at her closely. She was doing this to torture him. Obviously she was enjoying herself. "This is a whole other side to you I've never seen."

"Why should you?" She placed Justin in the back

and secured his seat. "You're always charging at me and biting my head off."

He thought of some of the barbs she'd delivered at his expense. If he was "biting her head off," it certainly didn't seem to cramp her style any. "Too bad it keeps growing back."

Mikky opened her door, then remembered that she had no idea what his address was. "Where is it you live? In case we get separated."

He paused, obviously debating the wisdom of having her come to his place. "You don't have to do this, you know."

They'd already been through this. "I have seven brothers and sisters, five of whom are younger than I am. I was the one who helped raise the others. What are your credentials?"

Tony blew out a breath. He supposed he could use the help. He could always call his aunt, but this might go over better if he thought through what he was going to say. Reluctantly he gave Mikky the address to the apartment complex where he was staying.

Tony unlocked the door, shouldering his way in first as he juggled three bags. Holding the baby, Mikky walked in behind him. She looked around very slowly. The small living room was crowded with large boxes that bore the stamp of a moving company's logo on their sides.

She turned toward Tony as he deposited his load on the small, square kitchen table. "How long ago did you say you'd moved here?"

"I didn't say." But she wanted to know, he thought in resignation, so he told her. "Two months, why?"

Two months. That meant he'd moved in just as the

project had started. Mikky wondered if that was why everything was still in boxes, or if there was another reason. Maybe he hadn't made up his mind to stay yet. Either that or he hated to unpack.

She shrugged. Justin began to fuss in earnest against her shoulder. "No reason, I just didn't think you were a slow mover, that's all." There were more boxes in the small hallway. Her guess was that they littered the entire apartment. She couldn't live like this. Clutter annoyed her. "Don't you like having things where you can find them?"

There were things in the boxes Tony wasn't up to going through yet. They were mingled with other, common, everyday items he'd learned to do without for the time being. But he didn't feel like explaining any of that to her. "Not particularly."

"I have no comeback for that."

"Thank God." He reached for Justin.

She took a step back. "Why don't you let me go on holding him while you unpack? Unless you want to leave the food where it is, too?"

He didn't particularly like the way she stuck her tongue into her cheek when she teased him. "You have a nasty streak a mile wide, you know that?"

She wandered into the bedroom. She was right, more boxes. "They tell me I grow on people."

He poked his head out of the kitchen. The last thing he wanted to do was to flatter her. "They lie."

"I'm not here to grow on anybody." She walked back into the kitchen. "I'm here to help a guy through the night."

He supposed that in her own, offbeat, irritating way, she meant well. "I'm sure the baby appreciates that."

"I was talking about you."

Chapter Four

"Where do you want this?"

Tony looked up from the groceries he was unpacking to see Mikky walking toward him. Emerging from the bedroom with Justin on her arm, she held out the diaper she'd just taken off the boy.

The aroma preceded it.

"As far away from here as possible." Grabbing the bag closest to him, he held it open under the soiled diaper. Mikky dropped it in, and he clamped the bag closed immediately, tying the two ends together tightly to momentarily help seal in the smell. He took it out to where the trash bin was located as quickly as possible.

Mikky watched him leave, amused. Justin made a noise against her shoulder. "I think he's just found something about you he isn't too crazy about," she whispered, brushing her cheek lightly against the baby's head. She loved the soft, downy feel of baby-fine hair. Loved, when she came right down to it, the very feel of babies themselves. "Who do you belong to, little man?'' she murmured. ''And why in heaven's name would they ever have given you up?''

Nothing, she knew, would ever have made her give up her own child. No matter what. But then, she had to look no further than in her own family to know that not everyone felt the way she did.

Tony returned, closing the door behind him. ''Mission accomplished?'' she teased. He looked so solemn. What did it take to lighten this man up?

He didn't bother answering. Instead, he crossed to her and looked at Justin. ''I don't remember them smelling that bad.''

It was on the tip of her tongue to say that if he'd ever changed diapers on a regular basis, he would know just how bad it could get. But something told her that any reference to his past as a father would only be scratching at a scab that hadn't fully healed.

So she shrugged nonchalantly, shifting the baby to her other side.

''You tend to forget that kind of thing, along with labor, they tell me.'' Although her sister Lisa could go on for hours about that—longer than she'd actually been *in* labor. ''Nature's way of ensuring that the species continues. Otherwise the line would have stopped with the first baby that Adam and Eve had—not that they had disposable diapers.''

A movement caught his eye. Shifting so that he was behind her, Tony looked at the baby. ''He's sucking up your shirt.''

Gently, he tried to disengage the rooting mouth from Mikky's shoulder. His fingers skimmed against her, and he felt the same unsettling sensation he'd felt earlier. The closest thing he could liken it to was static electricity, but the night was far from dry enough for that.

Tony didn't dwell on it. Some things were better off dismissed.

The sudden contact surprised Mikky. As did the edgy feeling that arrived in its wake. A little like discovering an unexpected kick to a harmless drink, she thought, turning so that she could face Tony.

Justin was back to working on her shirt. The wet spot was getting wider. With a firm grasp, she extracted the material again.

"That's because he's still hungry." She brushed a kiss to the top of the downy head. "C'mon, Justin, let's feed you something with a little less fiber in it."

Shifting the baby so that he now sat astride her hip, his legs dangling on either side, Mikky made her way back into the kitchen. It was a path not without its challenges.

"This is some obstacle course you have here." She glanced toward Tony. How could he *live* like this? Didn't he bump into things when he got up in the middle of the night? "You should at least push the boxes over against the walls."

What was it about her voice that instantly got his back up? "I appreciate the input," Tony informed her tersely. "I'd also appreciate it if you restricted your architectural forays to the high school."

Well, they seemed to have danced a full circle, Mikky thought, stopping. "That wasn't a foray, that was a point of common sense. As are most of our clashes over the design."

His eyes narrowed as they met hers. "And you'd be the one on the side of common sense."

Her smile was wide and triumphant—and almost adorable, if it hadn't been on her, Tony thought. "Now you're getting it."

He closed his eyes and sighed. "What I am getting is a headache."

"Headache?" Mikky laughed at the suggestion. Was he that delicate? Then for all his noble sentiments he was in for a big surprise. "Mister, you ain't seen nothing yet." She shifted so that the hip with Justin on it was higher than her other. "Wait until this little fella decides he wants to hold an all-night jam session and all you want to do is build a closer relationship with your pillow. *Then* you can talk about having a headache."

"Right now," Tony muttered under his breath, "I feel like I'm *with* a headache."

She couldn't make out what he was saying, but she thought it might be better that way. Finally making it into the kitchen, Mikky saw that the jars were all still on the counter. Tony had them lined up in a single row against the wall beside the sink. They were arranged by type. This was probably as close as he came to putting things away. At least he wasn't completely organizationally challenged, she mused.

She selected a jar and turned to look at him. "Should I feed him, or do you want to?"

Tony was surprised that she actually gave him the option. Maybe the woman did have some sense of decorum beneath that tough hide of hers. Because she'd thought to ask instead of assume, he deferred to her. All things considered, he was a little leery of doing this on his own. Since she was here, he could watch. And remember. "I'll let you do it since you're the pro."

Mikky wasn't sure if he was giving her a backhanded compliment or if his sarcasm was so well hidden, it had disappeared. With a grin, she gave him the benefit of the doubt. "You just want to put off getting messy as long as possible."

He inclined his head. "Okay, maybe there's that, too."

She looked around and found the baby spoon she'd remembered to get. Shrink-wrapped on a rectangular piece of cardboard with the picture of a baby on it, it was all but hermetically sealed. There was no way she was going to get that off with only one hand.

"Here," she held it up to him. "Impress me. Get the wrapper off."

He took the spoon from her. "Is that all it takes to impress you?" He gave the wrapper a tug. It remained intact.

"It'd be a start." Obviously he hadn't looked very closely. "You'd be surprised how hard those things are to take off without using a knife."

"Thanks for the tip," he muttered, taking a knife out of the drawer. Prying the edge under the spoon, he cut it loose.

A thank-you. Wow, there was hope for the man yet. Taking the spoon from him, she looked toward the stove. No kettle. Why didn't that surprise her? What did surprise her was the absence of anything resembling a coffeemaker.

"Got any hot water?"

Tony tried to make sense of the question. "You want tea?"

"No." She held the spoon up to underscore her request. "I want to sanitize the spoon."

"Right," he muttered. He took the utensil back. "I knew that."

"Of course you did." Because Justin was fussing

again, this time in earnest, she began to sway, hoping to distract him. "But tea does sound nice," she added.

The sparkle that came into her eyes a moment before she turned away sent another warm, undulating sensation snaking its way through him. Mentally shaking himself loose, Tony began rummaging through a box just off the kitchen.

"I'm going to have to go down to the convenience store for some tea," he told her.

Finding what he was looking for, he took the small saucepan out and filled it with water. Irritating or not, Mikky was going out of her way to help him. He hadn't figured out her motives yet, but he supposed getting her some tea was the least he could do to repay her. He placed the pan on the burner and set it on high.

Without losing a beat, she covered the pan. "It'll boil faster," she assured him. "If you don't have any tea, that's all right. I'm easy. I'll just take coffee."

He had his sincere doubts about her *ever* being easy. He shrugged indifferently at her change in selection. "Same trip."

Moving closer to him, Mikky looked at Tony quizzically. "You don't have any coffee, either?" Maybe he didn't believe in stimulants. Which meant he undoubtedly avoided the mirror, she decided. When he wasn't scowling like Zeus on Olympus, ready to fling down thunderbolts, the man was certainly stimulating to look at. He had a face one of her sisters might have referred to as knock-down, drop-dead gorgeous. "What do you drink in the morning?"

"Coffee. From the deli truck," he added, sensing her confusion. A wisp of steam curled up, squeezing out from beneath the rim of the lid. Taking the lid off, he passed the spoon through the water, then rinsed it to cool it off.

She shook her head. "I couldn't wait that long. If I don't get coffee into me first thing in the morning, my motor won't go."

Tony had a feeling she was sorely underestimating her motor. From what he'd observed, especially in the last hour, her so-called "motor" probably ran nonstop night and day. "I thought you said you liked tea."

"I do." Mikky selected a jar proclaiming itself to be a chicken-noodle dinner. "To relax with." She took the spoon from him. "But just holding this little darling is relaxing enough." Sitting down at the table, she settled Justin on her lap and started feeding him.

He couldn't help noticing that she looked as if she were right at home, holding the baby. There were other things he could be doing instead of watching her slip a small, sliver spoon into a rosebud mouth. But for the life of him, he couldn't remember what one of them was. So he stood, like some damn wooden statue, he thought, and watched her while bittersweet memories tried to break through and overwhelm him.

She raised her eyes to his. This time, her teasing smile seemed far less offensive and annoying. He was probably giving her too much credit, he thought.

"Taking notes?"

He shrugged, shoving his hands into his pockets because he didn't know what else to do with them. She had an uncanny knack of making him feel like a gangly teenager. "Just amazed that you can stay quiet for any length of time."

Mikky dipped the spoon into the jar. "You don't make it easy to like you, you know."

He frowned. He wasn't after her friendship. Just a

little cooperation in the workplace. "I wasn't aware that you felt the need to try."

Mikky wondered if he'd always been like this, or if the death of his family had turned him into this malcontent.

"I try to like everyone I work with. Makes life easier." She slipped in another spoonful and watched half of it come oozing out again as Justin closed his mouth a little too enthusiastically. Tiny noodles threatened to slide down his chin to accent the smiles on the barnyard animals dancing on his newly purchased bib. "You know what your problem is?"

"You?" he guessed.

"No," she answered evenly. "You've got this huge knot in your stomach, and you can't seem to get past it."

Yes, there was a knot in his stomach, Tony admitted. An unwieldy, overwhelming knot. There had been ever since he'd lost his world. And he didn't need her to tell him that. Smile vanishing, his face darkened. "Where do you get off, analyzing me?"

Mikky refused to acknowledge the anger she heard. If he didn't stop being angry, it was going to wind up poisoning him eventually. And that, she thought, would be a terrible waste.

"Not analyzing, just noticing. Given your present state, I don't see how anyone would have thought that you could do a good job raising this baby."

Suspicion crowded his brow as his eyes darkened. "What are you saying?"

Offhand, she could think of only one reason why the baby was left for him. One reason why a man who had no particular skills or aptitude for babies would eschew the traditional path and try to hang on to that baby.

"Are you sure that there's no chance at all that Justin might be yours?"

Tony didn't answer right away. Instead, he crouched in front of her and looked directly at Justin. Using the edge of the bib, he wiped off both cheeks. Justin smacked his lips impatiently, looking at the jar of baby food Mikky held in her hand.

"My guess is that he's maybe nine months old. Nine months before that, I was living with my wife and son in Denver." He rose to his feet, his eyes still on hers. He set his mouth hard. "Not that it's any business of yours, but I loved my wife. I didn't have anyone on the side—or the front or the back," he added, anticipating the kind of questions that might run through her mind. "Just her. I'm old-fashioned that way."

She smiled at the description. "Nice trait. Don't get annoyed, I was just trying to figure out why someone would single you out to leave a baby with."

This time the shrug was born of frustration. He'd already asked himself that several times. He had no answer. "Angelo and Shad seem like more likely candidates," he admitted. They both still had their children. And their wives.

"But they're not really on the site much," she pointed out. "And maybe whoever left the baby saw something in you that made them feel you were a better choice than simply abandoning Justin in a vacant lot."

That made him only a shade better than nothing. Leave it to her. "You sure know how to turn a man's head."

She grinned. "I call it as I see it."

"An honest woman." In a way he supposed she was, at that. At the very least, she didn't pull punches.

She slipped the last spoonful into the open, waiting mouth. "Something like that."

"Why wouldn't they have left him with you?"

She shrugged. "Who knows? Maybe they got our trailers mixed up, or maybe whoever it was was in a hurry. Or maybe they sensed you wouldn't turn to the police. I guess there's just no way knowing for sure without knowing who left the baby in the first place."

He suddenly realized that the jar was empty. "Hey, you finished."

"So I did." Retiring the spoon into the jar, Mikky placed both on the table and turned the baby around to face her. "Good job, Justin." Her eyes swept over him. Unless Tony changed his mind and turned him over to the police, Justin was going to need a change of clothes in the morning. "Of course, you're wearing about half your dinner, but hey, it's a start. Are you still hungry? Are you?" Holding him up, she nuzzled her head against the boy's tummy. Justin exploded with a laugh that surrounded her heart.

"Um, hold still a second."

Now what, didn't he approve of her playing with the baby? "Why?"

"He spit up a little in your hair." Tony had no idea what made him catch her hand as she started to feel around for the offending spot. Or what made him hold it a beat too long. It surprised him how small and delicate her hand felt. Did wolverines have delicate hands? "Not much," Tony added, releasing her hand. "Just that I didn't think you'd want to let it get stiff. Wait a minute." He took a paper towel and wet it, then crossed back to her. "Lean your head forward a little."

Stunned by this chivalrous turn, Mikky did as he asked and kept very still. She could smell his cologne, she realized. Funny, she hadn't noticed it before. Maybe because he didn't seem like the type to wear any.

If she was wrong about that, maybe she was wrong about other things about him as well.

"Okay, it's out." He tossed the towel toward the sink.

"Thank you," she murmured. Looking up at him, her eyes strayed to the clock that hung on the wall just behind him. At least he'd made some effort...

As if set to a thirty-second delay, the hour registered belatedly. Her eyes widened.

For just the briefest second, Tony felt himself trapped within them. And then she moaned and brought him back to reality. "What's the matter?"

"Oh, God, look at the time." Mikky was on her feet, although she couldn't exactly slam-dunk Justin and bolt. "Johnny's going to kill me." She'd meant to call him as soon as they'd arrived at Tony's apartment, but the thought had completely left her head.

"Boyfriend?" The idea of her being involved in any sort of male-female relationship caught Tony off guard. He would have thought her kind killed after mating. A tiny splotch of irritation surfaced for no reason. He banked it down.

"Brother," Mikky corrected. "Right now a very angry brother." She hated when she forgot things. She was the one who was supposed to be able to juggle everything, no matter how many of those things she had to keep up in the air at the same time. "He's standing in front of the Newport Theaters, waiting for me. We were supposed to see that new science fiction movie that's opening tonight." Their tastes in movies almost identical, she and Johnny saw all the new movies together. He'd been looking forward to this for weeks.

Her brother was going to be fit to be tied. She needed to page him.

"You like science fiction?" Tony couldn't picture her mesmerized by space aliens. But then, science fiction was a little out there and so was she.

"I *love* science fiction," she corrected. Placing Justin against her shoulder, she began to pat his back. A quirky grin Tony found unsettlingly diverting lifted the corners of her mouth. "When I was a kid, I could recite the dialogue from all three *Star Wars* movies."

"You must have been a great draw at parties," he muttered. He was trying to be flip, but if he were being honest, he would have had to admit that he could never get himself to pass up watching any of the famous trilogy if he was channel surfing. "Which one was your favorite?"

"Han Solo. I've got a real weakness for dashing adventurers who come through in a pinch."

Why did he feel as if she was directing that comment at him? "No, I mean of the three movies."

She flushed a little at her mistake. "Oh, the first one."

He'd liked the third. He couldn't help asking, "You don't like sequels?"

"The sequels were great, it's just that I like things when they're fresh with promise—" she continued as she patted Justin's back "—when everything is new. I don't like endings." Her voice drifted off.

Tony caught himself wondering about Mikky, thinking of her as something other than a walking tongue. Now there were questions linking up to one another in his head.

Was there a reason for her to feel that way? To hate

endings? Had there been an ending in her life, the way there had in his?

"Yeah," he agreed quietly. "Me, neither." He looked at Justin. His cheek pressed against her shoulder, Justin's eyes were slowly beginning to drift shut. "Think he's tired?"

"We could try putting him to bed—speaking of which," she raised her eyes to his, "where will that be?"

Tony hadn't thought that far ahead. Judging by the expression on her face, Mikky had probably guessed that, which brought back his feeling of annoyance. He found annoyance more comfortable than the unsettling one he'd just experienced.

He shrugged. "I could put him on my bed."

Mikky nodded. Sounded like a plan to her. Justin was too large to spend the night in an emptied-out drawer, the way two of her little brothers had when they'd made their debut one after the other and money had been too tight to afford another crib.

"That could work." She glanced around. "You certainly have no shortage of things you could surround the bed with." He was looking at her blankly. "You don't want to have him rolling off. Nothing fun about a midnight run to the emergency room."

A deaf man would have noticed the conviction in her voice, Tony thought. "You've made them?"

Mikky nodded. "More than once." Things always seemed so much scarier at night, as if the lack of sunlight automatically made conditions more serious. "We found out my sister Alexis was allergic to peanuts the hard way. We got her to the hospital just in time. And then there was Randy, the flying squirrel."

"You took a squirrel to the emergency room?"

Laughing, she realized there was no way for him to know. "That's just a nickname I gave one of my brothers—after he tried to climb out of his second-story window and meet his friends, when he should have been sleeping. Broke his arm in two places. Lucky he didn't break his neck, as well." She'd been so terrified, negotiating empty streets like a race car driver on his trial run at Indy, with Randy in the back seat, screaming the entire way. "Those were the nocturnal visits. I've had my share in the daytime, too."

Tony suspected she was being dramatic. "Where were your parents?"

"My father worked three shifts at a restaurant to try to keep clothes on our backs and food in our stomachs. The manager liked him so the food part wasn't as hard as it could have been." Her expression grew a little rigid around the edges. "Your guess is as good as mine as to where my mother was." Realizing that had sounded bitter, she cleared her throat. "Why don't you go and barricade your bed, and we'll see about putting this little guy down."

The momentary glimpse into her past made him uncomfortable. Unable to work his way through his own situation, he didn't know what to say when confronted with someone else's problems. That she'd given him a way out left him beholden to her. The tally appeared to be mounting up. His guess was that she'd probably call it in before the week was out.

"Right."

She nodded toward the wall phone in the kitchen. "Mind if I use your phone?"

He disappeared into his bedroom. "Help yourself."

Dialing Johnny's cell phone, Mikky mentally counted the number of rings. It went the full count. "Ten.

Damn." She frowned as she heard the recorded message. "He is too in range."

Curious, Tony came out again. She didn't sound as if she was talking to her brother. "Not there?"

Disgusted, Mikky hung up. "The connection's not there. I hate that cell phone recording—'The mobile unit you have dialed is not answering. It is either out of range or not on,'" she mimicked in a low, monotone voice, then groaned.

With a sigh she walked past Tony to the bedroom. "I swear, sometimes I think I could get a better connection if I just strung up two tin cans."

He followed her. "You'd need an awful lot of string for that."

He'd left a space open for her by the bed, she noted. Oversight, or thoughtful? She decided on the former. "Not a problem. I've got friends in all kinds of places." Gingerly she lowered the baby onto the bed, placing Justin on his back. When Tony reached for him, she caught his sleeve.

"What are you doing?"

There was that challenge again, Tony thought, as if no one could do anything right but her. "I'm going to turn him over on his stomach."

Still holding his sleeve, she shook her head. "Bad idea."

"All babies sleep on their stomachs."

"Not anymore. Latest studies show that babies run less of a risk of incurring SIDS if they sleep on their back." He raised a brow. "I also baby-sit for two nephews and a niece. I keep up on this kind of stuff."

She probably did at that. "Does anyone ever win an argument with you?"

In lieu of a blanket, she took one of the large, plush

bath towels from the bathroom and covered Justin with it. "Only when I'm wrong." Stepping back, she started to move another box in place.

Fool woman was going to get a hernia proving she was macho. Biting off a reprimand, Tony moved her out of the way and did the honors himself. The only way Justin was getting out of there was by pole vaulting. "How often is that, in your opinion?"

She looked up at him, straight-faced and innocent. "Anyday now."

He had a feeling she wasn't kidding.

Chapter Five

Tony waited until the low, murmuring sound of her voice had stopped before entering the kitchen. That he still heard a little of it in his head he attributed to the fact that she talked almost nonstop, not to the fact that the sound had somehow wound, seductively, into his blood and was even now unsettling him.

That just wasn't possible. Not with someone like Mikky.

"Did you get ahold of your brother?" He figured she'd reached someone, unless he'd heard her talking to a wrong number.

"Yes, finally." She replaced the receiver as she turned to face Tony. "Johnny's not too happy about missing the first evening show, but he'll forgive me. He always does."

Tony laughed shortly. She probably ruled the members of her family like a power-hungry despot. "Does he have any choice?"

"Sure." Another quirky smile played along her lips,

drawing his attention back to them. As much as he hated
to admit it, there was something about her smile that
got to him. "He can forgive me or die. I always leave
that option open to my relatives."

He had a feeling her relatives weren't the only ones
she included in that group. Diminutive, small-boned and
deceptively delicate looking, Michelle Rozanski, by his
reckoning, could still have been the poster woman for
the independent female of the '90s. She was the last
person he'd ever think of who needed to be taken care
of.

Light years away from Teri, he thought. Together
since they were freshmen in college, Teri had turned to
him for everything. Made him feel as if he were necessary to her very existence.

He missed being needed. Missed making a difference
in someone's life.

Maybe that was why he'd been so adamant about
keeping the baby until Justin's mother showed up. He
needed to feel that someone needed him. Even a face-
less woman with no name. And it was a cinch that the
baby needed him, at least for now.

"Well, I'd better get going." Mikky hesitated, looking at him. Debating. "You'll be all right?"

He wasn't accustomed to having his capabilities
questioned. "I'm not exactly helpless."

She sighed. "I didn't say that."

He narrowed his eyes. She was doing it again. Twist-
ing things so that it looked as if he were the one in the
wrong instead of her. Had she learned how to do that,
or did it come naturally to her?

"You didn't have to."

Humor, Mik, remember to keep your sense of humor,
she warned herself.

"Well, before we begin dissecting my overbearing personality again, I'll just get going." Unsure why she was lingering, she turned away and reached for the doorknob. "See you Monday morning. Drawing boards at thirty paces."

"Wait."

Mikky debated the wisdom of remaining one second longer than she already had. Reminding herself that she *did* have to work with Marino until she was confident that her designs were not being scrubbed, Mikky turned around. "What?"

When she looked like that, it was hard for Tony to push the words out. But he owed them to her, and he always paid every debt, no matter how small or how troublesome. "Thank you."

It took every effort Mikky possessed not to let her mouth drop open. So he could say the words out loud, after all, and even look as if he meant them. Faced with what passed as a silent apology for his manner, she relented. She'd never been one to hold a grudge once any effort was made to make amends.

"You're welcome." She paused, vacillating. He'd taken a step toward meeting her halfway and, judging from his sunny disposition, it hadn't been easy for him. "Here." On impulse, she opened her purse, took out one of her business cards and wrote on the back of it before handing it to him. "That's my home phone number. If you find yourself needing help, call me."

Tony took the card, his fingers brushing against hers. Something in him wanted the contact to widen, to grow. Lack of sleep had to be evaporating his brain.

His eyes met hers and held. "Why are you doing this?"

Mikky didn't like being questioned. Not when she

didn't even have any clear answers herself. A careless shrug marked her exit. "Just a sucker for a poor dumb animal, I guess."

She opened the door, and that was when they both heard it.

Wailing.

Mikky stopped and looked over her shoulder, not toward the sound, but toward Tony. He'd stiffened uneasily.

You've already done more than your share. This isn't any of your business.

Somehow she just couldn't make herself believe it wasn't. What was worse, she couldn't make herself leave. The fact that the baby might have started crying when she was safely in her car driving home, instead of now, and she would have been none the wiser for it didn't mitigate her feelings of guilt.

She couldn't leave him like this.

Calling herself an idiot, Mikky closed the door again.

Tony looked at her uncertainly. "What are you doing?"

Was it in her mind, or was there just the slightest touch of relief woven through his defensive tone? She tossed her purse back on the kitchen table. "The next showing doesn't start for another three hours. I guess staying a few more minutes wouldn't hurt."

Tony followed her into the bedroom. He didn't like the idea of being more indebted to her than he already was. But he liked the idea of being left alone with a wailing child even less, especially after dark. Somehow the cries seemed more plaintive in the absence of sunshine.

"Well," he said expansively, "if you have nothing else to do—"

They were getting into muddy water again. Mikky held up a hand to stop Tony before he went any further.

"Why don't we just leave it at 'thank you' and you can think of yourself as ahead of the game?" Shouldering one of the boxes aside so she could reach Justin, she picked the baby up. The wailing settled down to a heart-wrenching whimper. "What's the matter, big boy, did you have a bad dream?"

Patting the baby's bottom, she murmured something against his ear. Though he'd been listening, Tony couldn't quite make the words out. Mikky kissed the baby's forehead.

"Well, you're not wet, you're not warm and we did just feed you." She looked down at Justin. The redness in his cheeks was settling back to a rosy hue. "I think you just want attention, what do you think?"

It almost sounded as if she were carrying on a conversation with the infant. "Are you waiting for him to answer you?"

She shifted Justin to her shoulder. "Oh, he's answering me, all right. Babies have their own way of communicating." Mikky spared Tony a glance. "Too bad some of them lose that knack when they grow up."

They were on the brink of another sharp-tongued exchange; he could feel it. But she was going out of her way, so he curbed the response that rose to his lips. "What do you want me to do?"

He'd only get in her way, and there were enough things in the way within the room as it was. Mikky nodded toward the tiny hallway and the living room beyond. "Why don't you go and unpack?"

He shoved his hands deep into the back pockets of his jeans. "Why do those boxes bother you so much?"

There had been eight of them, not counting her father,

stuffed into a small apartment with only two bedrooms. She'd grown up in cramped quarters despite all her best efforts to keep things neat. The state of Tony's apartment brought it all back to her, reminded her of the harder times, where not only money but space was at a premium.

But that was all far too personal to share with a man who couldn't care less about her background. "Clutter bothers me."

"I guess being around construction sites must be hell for you."

Mikky ignored the sarcasm and took his comment at face value. "That's different. That's clutter on its way to becoming something." Because Justin was still whimpering, she began rocking him. "What you have here is just clutter."

She was right about that, but Tony wasn't about to let her know that. "Thanks for pointing out the difference."

He left the room before things began to escalate again.

It was several minutes later, as he debated unpacking at least a couple of the boxes in the living room—in the interest of space and not because she was harping on it—that he became conscious of the sound of her voice, low and melodic, drifting around him. Surrounding him like a large, warm towel just freshly taken from the dryer. It took effort to shake off the effects.

Tony glanced at the pile of papers on the coffee table. Even though he'd brought some work home with him, he felt too restless to concentrate and focus on anything with her here. Mindless physical activity seemed like the perfect solution.

He approached the boxes closest to him. Except that

it wouldn't be mindless. Everything within the boxes had some sort of memory attached to it, however minor. He didn't feel up to dealing with them yet.

Hearing her sing tipped the scales. The boxes could wait a little longer. He had enough space to navigate from room to room, and he didn't need her telling him what he should or shouldn't do.

Straining, he tried to hear what Mikky was singing. But he couldn't make out any of the words. There was a reason for that, he suddenly realized. She wasn't singing in English. It was some foreign tongue he couldn't put a label on. All he knew for certain was that it wasn't Spanish, which he knew enough of to recognize.

This was probably just gibberish.

For gibberish, the slow, sad tune had a hypnotic power. He tried to shut out the sound and found that was even harder to do than deciphering the words. Her voice was low, seductive, tantalizing. Like light wine that teased and aroused before it went in for the kill and intoxicated.

Silly thought. Where was he getting all this from?

He was just tired, he thought. Maybe before he did anything else, he'd just stretch out in front of the television set and watch the news for a few minutes. Or see whatever else was on.

It bothered him that he was out here while she was in there, tending to the baby that had so quickly become his personal responsibility. But if he went in, they were sure to get into it again.

He wasn't up to arguing.

Turning on the set, he waited two beats before changing the channel. And giving the next contender the same time limit. What was it about her that irritated him so? he wondered. After all, Mikky seemed like a decent

enough woman, giving up her evening to help someone
she didn't get along with. And God knew she wasn't
hard on the eye, if he were in the market for that sort
of thing. The curves were all in the right places, and
she had a way of raising her breasts when she was making a particularly salient point....

Best not go there. He flipped through two channels
in quick succession, working his way into the cable se-
lections.

It was her mouth that was the problem, he decided.
If she just kept it shut...if he thought about it, it was
almost tempting when it was shut....

He stopped surfing.

"Well, he's finally asleep."

A bone-weary sigh followed her statement. Walking
out of the bedroom, Mikky felt exhausted. It had taken
more than a full hour of rocking and pacing, making a
zigzag pattern between the boxes that threatened to
make her dizzy after a while, before she had finally
gotten Justin to drift off again. For a while there, it had
been almost touch-and-go which of them would fall
asleep first.

"I'm just going to—"

Mikky stopped as she realized that Tony hadn't acknowledged her entrance, not because of any habitual
crustiness on his part but because he was asleep himself.
Sprawled out on the sofa, with every indication that
he'd slid down from a sitting position, he was sound
asleep. Though the program on the television screen
was going strong, it was there by happenstance instead
of choice. The remote had fallen from his slack fingers.

For a moment Mikky just stood there looking at him.
Asleep, Tony didn't look nearly as forbidding as he did

awake. His hair had fallen into his eyes, and his features had softened under the light hand of sleep. He really was heart-stoppingly handsome, at that, she mused. It was his perpetual scowl that made her more or less oblivious to his looks. Well, maybe less than more, she amended, a smile creeping to her lips.

"You don't look so much like the big, bad wolf anymore, Marino," she murmured. She curbed the desire to trail her fingers through the wayward locks of his hair.

Now what, she wondered. By all rights she could just slip out and go, but she didn't feel right about leaving the baby alone while Tony was asleep out here. What if he slept like a dead man? What if the baby started to cry and he didn't hear him? Tony hadn't woken up when she'd come out talking to him, and he was sleeping right through the rather loud program.

Not her problem.

Yeah, it was, she amended. She was here, that made it hers.

Someday she was going to have to do something about anesthetizing that conscience of hers.

"Damn, but you don't make this easy, Marino." Making up her mind, she went to the telephone in the kitchen. She had to page Johnny again.

And while she was at it, maybe she'd put in a call to Thad. Eleven months her junior and Johnny's twin, Thad had just made detective on the narcotics squad of the Bedford Police Department. If anyone could find things out for her, it was Thad.

The ache in his neck and shoulders seeped into his consciousness, mingling with fading strains of a woman's voice that echoed in his head and displacing it. It was a dream.

At least the voice was. The ache was real.

Tony stretched, trying to work the kink out. He must have dozed off.

As his surroundings penetrated the lifting fog around his brain, he realized that the television set was off. And instead of darkness, there was daylight spilling in through the windows.

When did that happen? He didn't even remember closing his eyes.

"Damn."

Blinking away the last haze of sleep, he looked at his watch. His annoyance elevated. He'd not only allowed himself to fall asleep, but he'd been sleeping for almost eight hours.

Justin.

Tony shot to his feet and almost tripped when he took a step. There was a blanket bunched at his feet. It had fallen off him when he'd bolted upright. But he didn't remember...

Unless she...

Confused, Mikky's name ricocheted through his brain like a misfired shot. Right now, she didn't matter. He'd left a baby alone, he upbraided himself as he picked his way to his bedroom as fast as possible.

She was right about these stupid boxes, too, damn her.

The baby wasn't alone.

Mikky was curled at the foot of the bed, her arm tucked beneath her head as an impromptu pillow. He felt something stir within him as he looked at her, wrapped in sleep. It had been a long time since he'd watched a woman sleep.

Tony roused himself. She looked far from comfortable. How long had she been here like this?

Obviously all night, and that was his fault. He was going to hear about it the minute she woke up. But that didn't matter right now. What did was Justin. He looked toward the little boy and found to his relief that the baby was still sound asleep, just like she was.

The best of all possible worlds.

Until she woke up, Tony thought, easing out of the room.

Mikky woke up with a start, unsure what it was that had awakened her. Disoriented, she tried to remember where she was and why. For a few seconds she thought she was back in Los Angeles, in the rundown apartment on Beaker Street. Sharing a bed with Rebecca.

And then it came back to her. That's right, she was playing angel of mercy. For a devil of a man.

Time to get her wings refitted, she thought.

Very carefully, watching the baby to make sure she didn't accidentally jostle him, Mikky eased herself off the bed. This morning, she promised herself as she rotated her neck, Marino was on his own. She had a life to get back to.

Picking up the shoes she'd kicked off hours ago, she tiptoed out of the room and closed the door behind her. She was dying for a shower, but that was going to have to wait until she got home. There was no way she was taking one here. All she needed was to have Marino wake up and walk in on her. He would probably accuse her of attempting to seduce him.

As if that would even cross her mind. Cold day in hell before that would happen....

She wondered if Thad had found out anything, then realized it was too soon for that.

Tony wasn't where she'd left him. Calling out his name softly got her no response. He wasn't there.

"Terrific."

Maybe he'd decided the baby was a hot potato, and it was her turn to be "it." With a sigh, she ran her hand through her hair, trying to focus her brain.

She needed caffeine. Badly.

Maybe Marino had only been kidding about not having any coffee. Right now she would have settled for chewing on the unground beans.

She found neither.

Obviously, she thought, looking into the refrigerator, the man wasn't given to understatement. There was nothing inside except for the two cartons of milk she'd had him buy. Disgusted, she let the door drop. Curiosity pushed her to take inventory of the pantry. The jars of baby food were still on the counter. The cupboard yielded a half-empty box of breakfast tarts and some popcorn packages for the microwave. Toaster tarts and popcorn. That, she supposed, was his idea of a hot meal.

Mikky shook her head as her stomach growled. It had been hours since she'd eaten. The baby food was beginning to look pretty good to her.

No wonder Marino was so grumpy. She would be, too, without something decent to eat.

The sound of a key being inserted into the lock had her whirling toward the front door. Relief outweighed annoyance when she saw Tony walking in. That meant the responsibility for the small human being in the bedroom had reverted back to him.

She looked around for her purse, then remembered

she'd tossed it on the table. It had slid down to the floor. "I thought maybe you decided to make a run for it."

Tony had no idea why that sounded as if she were talking like this was the morning after a passion-laced but meaningless night of torrid lovemaking. He dismissed the thought with effort.

"No, I just went out to get this." Opening the bag he'd brought with him, he took out a large takeout cup of coffee and placed it on the table in front of her. She didn't take it. "Do you want it in a mug?"

She looked at him in surprise and wonder. A smile began to curve her mouth. "It's for me?"

"Yeah, you said you couldn't get started in the morning without it." Shrugging, he looked away. He liked it better when she was swiping at him. He didn't know what to do with gratitude. "I thought—"

He'd been listening to her, Mikky thought. More than that, he'd remembered. She didn't know whether to be astonished or touched. When it came down to it, she felt a little of each.

Taking a long, big sip, she let the coffee wind its healing liquid all through her. "You do have your human moments, don't you?"

"Mostly not around you."

If she didn't know any better, she would have said he was being positively shy. "I noticed."

Tony nodded toward the bag. "There's an order of scrambled eggs in there. I don't know if you have a thing about cholesterol..." That was the singularly most stupid thing he'd ever said, he thought. It was her mouth again, throwing him off by smiling that way at him.

What would that quirky smile feel like if he— He stopped his mind from wandering too far.

"Right now the only thing I have 'a thing' about is

hunger. I'm starving." Like a child at Christmas, she gleefully looked into the bag and pulled out the order of scrambled eggs. "Thanks."

She ate with pleasure, he noticed. Like someone who thought food was a gift. Absently he wondered if that was a holdover from her childhood. He told himself there was no need to know, but he wondered, anyway.

"What was that I heard you singing to Justin last night?" He could swear that he could still hear it right now.

So he'd been listening. Mikky hadn't realized her voice had carried. She'd tried to be quiet. "An old Polish lullaby. I don't know all the words, just a couple of refrains actually, but it sticks in my head, and it seems to do the trick with babies. I sang it to all my brothers and sisters when they were little."

Tony could see her doing that, holding court amid a group of small children. He supposed she had a nice voice as far as singing went. "Did your mother sing it to you?"

The open expression on her face darkened just a touch. "I really don't remember."

She did, he thought, but she didn't want to talk about it. It was too private. He could respect that.

Too bad it wasn't a two-way street.

But then, that didn't matter either, really. It wasn't as if they were going to be running into each other very much after this. Once the high school was on its way to completion, Tony doubted they'd ever see each other again. But for now, Tony thought as he lingered over his coffee, it felt nice having someone to share the table with.

Chapter Six

"I didn't mean to sack out on you like that."

Tony found it easier to address the air above her head than to look directly at her when he spoke. It was the coward's way he supposed, but he chose to think of it as taking a rational approach. This way there'd be no temptation to get into an argument with her when he was trying to apologize.

No temptation at all. But he knew Justin was his responsibility, not hers. He had to admit he was surprised Mikky hadn't upbraided him for shirking.

"You were tired."

Since she was being civil about it, he supposed he could be the same about other things. "Look, maybe we got off on the wrong foot before."

Mikky set down the container of eggs and studied him. He looked as if he'd spent an even-less-comfortable night on that chair than she had at the foot of the mattress.

"Besides," Mikky continued magnanimously,

"you're not the first person to bite off more than he could chew."

Another crack. Tony should have known better. The woman wasn't being civil, she was just lulling him into a false sense of security so she could set him up.

"And then again," he rescinded, "maybe we didn't. I'm not biting off anything." He resented the way she could just arbitrarily lump him into any category that pleased her fancy, as if he were nothing more than a laboratory rat, there for her observation and amusement. "I'm minding a baby for a friend."

Because he'd gotten her coffee, Mikky let his raised voice slide. Besides, she was too curious to have him stop talking now. Just where was he going with this? They'd already established that he didn't know who the baby belonged to. Had he lied?

"Who?"

The words had just popped out. Tony had no real friends out here anymore, outside of the family. He'd declined every invitation from the crew to grab a drink at a local restaurant after hours; had done everything he could to maintain a firm distance between himself and the others who worked for him. His heart wasn't into socializing; it was buried back in Colorado.

"A friend who'll remain nameless until they show up," he snapped at her. "What are you, a part-time interrogator for the CIA?"

"If I were," she informed him tersely, getting up, "you would have been blown up by now." Picking up the coffee cup, she threw back her head and drained its contents, then replaced it on the table. "I think the fat lady has just sung. Thanks for the coffee." With a sweep of her hand, she cleared away the two containers, depositing them into the wastebasket he had against the wall. "I'll see you at work."

But as she turned to go, Tony caught her wrist, upbraiding himself even as he did it. He wasn't even sure why he was trying to stop her, except that deep inside he knew he'd just behaved like a belligerent jerk. There was no question about it, she definitely brought out the worst in him.

Mikky looked at him, her mouth firmly shut, her eyes sweeping from his fingers wrapped around her wrist to his face. She waited for an explanation.

What was it about her eyes that got to him? That made him feel as if he was completely transparent when even he couldn't figure himself out? He hadn't a clue. "I wasn't always such an idiot."

Mikky contained a sigh before it escaped. Damn it, another veiled apology. Why couldn't Marino leave her in peace, let her embrace her annoyance and be done with it? When he made apologetic noises like this, she felt bound to let what he'd said earlier pass.

She was beginning to feel like a yo-yo.

She let her wrist drop. He loosened his hold. "Nice to know there's hope for humanity." Feeling a need for some sort of truce, and knowing it was up to her to initiate it, she searched for common ground between them. "Why don't we just agree that we seem to rub each other the wrong way and let it go at that?" Then, lest her words instigate another volley, for whatever mysterious reason he might see fit, she added, "I've seen enough to convince me that you can be nice when you want to be. I just seem to set you off, that's all."

It was silently understood that he reciprocated the reaction.

On impulse Mikky rose on her toes to brush a kiss on his cheek.

Surprised by the sudden movement, Tony turned his head just enough for the kiss to miss its mark. And find a completely unexpected one.

Surprise built on surprise, utterly overwhelming him. Knocking him to his knees, figuratively if not literally.

Maybe it was because his resistance was low. Maybe it was because he hadn't kissed a woman since the morning Teri left his life so abruptly.

Most likely, he thought later, it was because Michelle Rozanski was an anomaly of nature that the world hadn't been able to categorize yet. An anomaly that knocked the wind out of everything she encountered.

But whatever the reason, the upshot was that he suddenly found himself falling, headfirst, into a vortex that was like a multicolored funnel without beginning or end. He wasn't even totally sure he was going to come out of it alive.

Wow. That was all Mikky could think of. *Wow.*

The man kissed every bit as well as he looked as if he might—which was a hell of a whole lot. Somewhere in the recesses of her mind, she'd known he would. The sensation his kiss generated was like opening an oven door and being hit with a sudden blast of heat. She felt her edges turning crisp.

It came up all around her, surrounding her, sizzling her toes, singeing her body. *You know what happens when you play with fire,* a little voice taunted her. It didn't matter, she could be brave.

Belatedly Mikky realized she had stopped breathing.

Tony couldn't remember putting his arms around her, couldn't remember pulling her closer or deepening a kiss that was already fathomless. But somehow he found himself sealed to her, feeling his pulse racing away to parts unknown, along with his sense of orientation.

Holding her the way he might have once held Teri.

The memory of Teri abruptly ended the moment for him. He pulled his head back. "I didn't mean— I—"

Lips barely able to move, Mikky held up her hand to stop his halting excuse midstream. There was no need to put into words what they were both feeling. It had been a mistake, a huge mistake. The less said about what had just happened, the better. They still had to maintain a working relationship come Monday morning, and this could really mess things up even more than they already were.

What had she been thinking? She'd been wondering somewhere in the back of her head what it might feel like to have him kiss her. That had just been perverse curiosity. She certainly hadn't expected to feel like this about it. As if someone had just set a torch to the known universe.

Why couldn't someone she liked ever have kissed her that way?

"Same here." The words came out in a harsh whisper, forcing their way up a throat she discovered had gone dry as sawdust.

Seconds later, the doorbell rang, making them spring apart as if they'd just been catapulted to opposite ends of a war zone.

Welcoming the diversion, Tony pulled open the door. Still disoriented and trying desperately to get his bearings, he tried to focus on Angelo standing on his doorstep.

Had he forgotten about something?

Tony *really* looked out of it, Angelo thought. He

would have said that he'd gotten him out of bed, except that his cousin was still wearing the clothes he'd had on yesterday.

What gives? he wondered.

"Hi." Not waiting for an invitation, Angelo walked in. "I know it's early, but I just wanted to stop by to see how you were doing. Oh. Oh."

The second "oh" was followed by a wide, sheepish grin as Angelo saw Mikky standing just to the left of the door and Tony. She had that same, slightly dazed look that was on his cousin's face. They both looked as if they'd just jumped off a wild amusement park ride. Things began to dawn. Talk about bad timing.

Angelo began backing away. "Obviously you're doing better than I thought you were. Sorry, I didn't mean to interrupt anything."

Reacting, Tony grabbed his cousin's arm before Angelo could make it out the door. That's all he needed, for Angelo to get the wrong idea about what he was seeing. Word would spread like wildfire through the family. Angelo wasn't exactly closemouthed.

"You're not interrupting anything," Tony told him emphatically.

A wail burst into the room, loud enough to sound as if it was right there with them instead of coming from the bedroom.

Stunned, Angelo looked from Mikky to Tony. "Is that a—?"

Taking a deep breath as she finally pulled herself together, Mikky nodded. "Yes."

Angelo's eyes narrowed as he turned toward his cousin. He lowered his voice, inclining his head so that Mikky was momentarily shut out. "You know, as I recall, when we were growing up you worked fast, but not *this* fast.''

Tony made an unintelligible noise. "It's not mine, you numbskull.''

"I see family affection runs deep here,'' Mikky observed to Angelo.

"Whose baby is it?'' Angelo finally asked, appearing confused.

"That,'' Mikky announced, looking at Tony even though she was talking to Angelo, "is the sixty-four-thousand-dollar question.''

"The what?'' Tony asked shortly.

"It was an old game show. Big scandal in its time. Allison likes to play trivia,'' Angelo explained, when Tony stared at him as if he'd left his senses.

Tony snorted. "Well, at least I have someone who can translate for her.'' Was that a normal cry? Or had Justin hurt himself? Without another word, he hurried to the bedroom.

Mikky was right on his heels.

"How about translating for me?'' Angelo called after him. "Last I checked, you didn't have a baby in this warehouse you call an apartment.'' Following them, he walked straight into a seven-foot tower and nearly sent the boxes crashing. He steadied it at the last moment, but just barely. "Damn it, Tony, haven't you done anything about these boxes yet?''

"Doesn't look that way, does it?'' Tony shot back dryly.

"I tried to tell him he should unpack, but he won't listen.''

"He never did. Even as a kid, you could never tell Tony anything. He always knew best.''

Hand on the doorknob, Tony turned to look at his

cousin accusingly. Why did he get the feeling he was outnumbered? "Hey, I'm standing right here."

"Couldn't miss you if we tried," Mikky quipped. Reaching past him, she put her hand over his and turned the knob, opening the bedroom door. Their eyes met for just a second, both aware that they were valiantly trying to ignore something in the making.

Angelo walked in first, then stopped dead when he saw the baby lying on the worn comforter.

"Okay." Angelo swung around to face both of them, but mainly looked to Tony. "What the hell's going on here?"

Where did he begin, Tony wondered, and how did he present it so that Angelo didn't give him any flack? He'd had about all he could put up with. "With what?"

"Where did the baby come from and, no offense," the remark was directed at Mikky, "but what is *she* doing here? I thought you two didn't get along."

"We don't," they said in unison with a volley of feeling.

Angelo threw up his hands. "Well, that explains nothing."

Kissing Mikky seemed to have short-circuited his brain, Tony thought in disgust. He couldn't seem to think clearly. "We don't know whose baby it is. I found it—and a note—on the trailer's doorstep last night after you and Shad left."

Angelo looked at his cousin incredulously. It sounded like something out of a movie made for television. "You're kidding."

Moving the barrier aside, Tony leaned over the bed and picked up the crying baby. "Does this look as if I'm kidding?"

Tony knew Angelo had always been a sucker for babies. His cousin took the small hand in his. The baby reciprocated by grasping one of Angelo's fingers in its grip.

He glanced at Tony suspiciously, his finger still firmly held captive. "And you have no idea—"

"None," Tony said, cutting off a second volley of questions.

"I think he needs changing." Moving between the two men, Mikky took Justin into her arms.

Angelo stood back, watching as Mikky confidently worked with the baby.

"He's going to need more clothes," Mikky said, handing the soiled diaper to Tony.

"Why didn't you call the police?" he asked Mikky.

Walking back into the room, Tony caught the question. "Don't you start."

Angelo looked at him. "What start? I just asked a simple question. The normal assumption would be that if you find a baby, you call the police."

That was her point, or had been last night, Mikky thought, picking up the baby from the bed. But after pacing the floor and rocking Justin for over half the night, she was finding it increasingly difficult to remain detached.

"Someone abandoned—" she began to explain.

"—temporarily left," Tony corrected, sending her a dark look.

He'd have to do better than that to intimidate her, she thought. "—this baby, and he—" she nodded toward Tony "—thinks he's just holding it for the mother or father until they have a change of heart."

Angelo had always had a soft heart, softer than his, Tony thought. He appealed to it now. He didn't really feel the need to have anyone siding with him, but it wouldn't exactly hurt, either. Someone who could drown out Mikky's incessant talking would be nice.

"If the police are called in, there'll be charges filed against the mother and then she won't be able to take care of the baby."

"You're assuming she'll come back," Mikky countered. "What if she doesn't?"

Tony took the baby from her. "If she doesn't, I'll think about that when the time comes."

Angelo frowned. They both seemed to have completely forgotten he was standing in the room. Though he knew it was a good sign that Tony had emerged out of his shell to show concern for someone else, he worried that there would be nothing but more heartache ahead for his cousin. One way or another, the baby was going to be taken from him, and from the looks of it, Tony'd already grown attached to it.

"But—" Mikky began.

"End of discussion," Tony informed her. "And while you're at it, lower your voice. You're going to upset Justin."

Angelo's mouth dropped open. This was bad. "You named him Justin? Tony—"

Tony recoiled from the pity he heard in Angelo's voice. "I didn't name him Justin. His name *is* Justin. It was on the note." Angelo glanced toward Mikky, who nodded. "What are you looking at her for? Don't you believe me?"

"It's not that I don't believe you, Tony. It's just that I'm worried."

"Well, go worry somewhere else. I'm fine. Go home, Angelo, I'm fine," he repeated with ferocity when Angelo didn't move.

Which just told Angelo that he wasn't fine at all. Angelo looked at Mikky with a silent plea in his eyes.

Though she looked reluctant about it, after a beat she acknowledged the plea with a slight nod. Relieved, Angelo withdrew.

Mikky took Justin from Tony as they heard the front door being closed. "We're all glad you're so fine, but it's time to feed this big guy before he starts in gnawing on that meathead of yours."

They began arriving less than an hour later.

Seeing that Angelo had returned, Tony opened the door before the doorbell set Justin off again. Tony was only mildly surprised to see his cousin. And to see that he wasn't alone. He'd brought Allison and the triplets. At two and a half, the triplets had enough energy to make a person believe that an invasion surpassed only by Dunkirk on D-Day took place each time they charged into a room. They charged past Tony now.

Tony nodded a greeting to Allison before looking at Angelo. "I see I didn't hurt your feelings enough to make you stay away."

Angelo laughed. "Hurt my feelings? I grew up with you, remember? You were born ornery and then got worse. I'm used to it."

Far from having his feelings insulted, Angelo had retreated merely to call together reinforcements. If Tony felt the need to play guardian angel to the abandoned baby, then they were going to back him up as best as they were able. Things, Angelo's mother had told all of them time and again, always had a way of working themselves out. Some things just took longer than others. And it was up to family to help "things" along their way.

"I brought some clothes you might need," Allison told Tony. "It's a loan," she added. "Dottie's going to be needing them in a while."

Angelo stopped dead. This was news to him. "Dottie? She's not—"

"She seems to think she is," Allison replied, a smile dimpling her mouth.

In his enthusiasm, since Tony was closest to him, Angelo slapped him on the back. "This is great. Guess we have something to celebrate. Am I supposed to know?" he asked Allison suddenly.

"As if you could ever keep a secret," she hooted. "Boys, be careful! You'll knock something over." She looked at Tony. "Why haven't you unpacked yet?"

He closed his eyes. Another county heard from. "I'm getting to it."

By noon Tony's apartment was filled to bursting with members of the extended Marino-McClellan-Delaney family. Shad and J.T. came next, bringing food and a portable crib as well as Frankie, Tina and Lily.

"Where are you going to put this?" J.T. asked as Shad brought in the portable crib. "Tony, you just have to get rid of these boxes."

"I think they're neat," Tina, a pint-size tomboy through and through, declared. She was already playing guerrilla soldier with the triplets.

J.T. leveled a look aimed at Tony. "I rest my case."

"Could you just imagine if she were a lawyer instead of an accountant?" Shad interjected, stealing a kiss as soon as he set down the crib.

Tony observed the playfulness between his cousins and their spouses with a bittersweet feeling weaving through him. It reminded him how good things could be.

And how much he missed having the life they were enjoying.

Bridgette Marino arrived last. There were tears in Bridgette's eyes when she walked in.

"Aunt Bridgette, what—" Tears always undid him. He looked helplessly at Dottie.

"Don't mind Mom. I just told her we were increasing the ranks by one."

"You know," Angelo commented, "we keep this up and we can declare ourselves a separate country pretty soon."

"At least a separate state," Mikky murmured. There seemed to be children everywhere.

Drying her eyes, Bridgette looked around. "Tony, you need a good woman to help you clean this all up. Lucky for you, there are several right here. We'll get to work after you show me this baby everyone is telling me about."

Dutifully, Tony took his aunt into the bedroom.

Mikky mused as he disappeared from view how in certain ways, Tony's family reminded her of her own.

She didn't have a sharp-tongued, softhearted mother like Angelo's, but she'd had her father, and for all his gruffness and the hours he'd spent working away from home, he'd still been the best father in the world as far as she was concerned. He'd given her and her siblings far more than food and shelter. He'd given his heart. His selfless love and sacrifice had helped her make her way through life, helped her shoulder whatever burdens happened along and made her feel lucky to be able to do so.

Even when it meant butting heads with someone the likes of Tony Marino.

Well, she saw that he had enough willing people to help him. There was no reason for her to remain any longer. It was the perfect time to retreat.

But she found her path obstructed by a woman who barely topped five feet. Dark, flashing eyes took measure of her quickly. "You are Michelle, yes?"

"Yes, but people call me Mikky."

"Mikky is a boy's name." The dark eyes swept over her again. "You are very much a woman. Tony tells me you helped him."

She was surprised that Tony had given her any acknowledgment at all. "I tried."

Bridgette nodded, pleased. "Trying is the first step to succeeding. Come, you help me now, yes?"

"Um...sure. With what?"

Bridgette merely smiled at her. "With whatever it is that needs to be done."

So she stayed, forgetting about the blueprints she'd promised herself to go over. Finding herself drawn into the heart of a family that didn't know how to take no for an answer.

"Oops, sorry." Turning abruptly, a tall, muscular young man nearly hit Mikky with an oversize box he was trying to move.

The steady influx of information from Bridgette allowed Mikky to know that she'd almost been knocked down by Shad's stepson, J.T.'s son from her first marriage.

When he flashed his smile, Frankie looked as if he had not only Shad's name as his own, but his blond hair as well, Mikky thought.

Trying to avoid the box in his arms, Mikky stumbled into Tony. The latter caught her before she could fall down. He pulled her up abruptly, her body brushing hard against his.

"Watch yourself, boy." The admonishment carried very little conviction. Not when Tony's attention was centered on the sensation that was telegraphing itself through every nerve ending in his body as he found her against him for the second time that day.

This time, the blame couldn't be ascribed to static

electricity. This time, if he was to be honest with himself, he'd have to reexamine things from another direction.

He decided that there were instances when honesty was highly overrated. Sleeping dogs were best left in exactly the condition they were found.

Releasing her, Tony blew out a breath. What *was* it about this woman that made him feel as if he'd just stepped into a puddle of water and grasped a live wire?

This had to stop, Mikky told herself. She was behaving like some addled adolescent girl. Moving back, she searched for something to say that would keep Tony from realizing that their brief encounter had sent torpedoes of excitement through her.

"It's nice to see that you can be bullied by your family." When he raised an eyebrow in a silent query, she gestured toward the activity. "The unpacking."

He lifted a shoulder. "Nobody stands a chance against Aunt Bridgette. She keeps after you until she gets her way. It's easier just to say yes." His eyes shifted toward her. "You two probably have a lot in common."

His smile was quick, sending another flash of electricity through her before she could steel herself from it. "I believe that's the nicest thing you've ever said to me."

"Yeah," he muttered evasively. "It probably is. Don't let it go to your head." With that, he walked away.

There went a man who would never be accused of having a silver tongue, she mused with a shake of her head. Hell if she knew what the attraction was.

But it was there, all the same.

Chapter Seven

Kicking off her shoes as she walked into her kitchen, Mikky pressed number three on the automatic dialer of her portable telephone. She shifted the receiver from one hand to the other as she shrugged out of her denim jacket, listening to the ringing on the other end.

"Narcotics, Detective Rozanski."

Thad's voice always sounded deeper over the telephone. At times it was hard to reconcile that deep voice with the little boy who'd always begged her to leave the light on because he was afraid of the dark. Now he was six foot four, and the dark was afraid of him, she thought with a smile.

"Hi, Thad, it's Mikky. Have you found anything out for me yet?" She undid the buttons of her shirt quickly, eyeing the bathroom in the distance. If she didn't take a shower soon, she was going to leap out of her skin.

There was a patient sigh on the other end. "Mikky, you only called me yesterday. I'm good, but I'm not that good."

She draped the shirt over the back of the sofa. "I always said that about you, little brother."

He laughed and then paused, debating getting into a futile conflict. But he had to try.

"Mikky—"

She straightened, alert. She'd thought long and hard before turning to Thad with this. Marino had trusted her with a secret. For the best of reasons, she'd bent that trust. But she wasn't about to break it.

"I know that tone, Thad." Her voice grew serious. "This is strictly off the record, do you understand? We're not even having this conversation."

"And while we're not having this conversation, do you want to tell me again why this guy hasn't come forward with the baby?"

She hadn't gone into it with him last night, asking only that he trust her and look into the matter for her. She appealed now to the good-hearted, sunny-faced boy she helped raise. For a good chunk of their lives, she'd been more his mother than his sister, even though she was only eleven months older.

"He's been through a lot, Thad. His wife and son were killed in a car crash a year ago. Drunk teenager, out joyriding. Marino didn't cope very well with the loss." Unsnapping her beige jeans, she stepped out of them. "I gather that this is the first signs of being human he's exhibited since the accident. He wants to help." Mikky picked up her jeans and sent them to join her shirt on the back of the sofa. "He really thinks that the mother will show up to take the baby back."

Thad could understand the motive, but it was still against his better judgment. "Abandonment's a crime, Mik."

"'The quality of mercy is not strained, it fall—'"

"Don't quote Shakespeare at me, Mik, just promise me that this isn't going to somehow come back to haunt me. I really like being a cop."

She knew that. It was all he'd ever wanted to be. She wasn't making the request of him lightly. "I promise."

"I feel better already," he quipped dryly. Then a note of seriousness entered his voice. "You never broke your promise to anyone."

She felt it was a point of honor not to. "Keeper of the flame, that's me." Taking a fresh towel from the linen closet, she slung it over her shoulder and made her way to the bathroom. "Look, I gotta go. Call me if you find anything."

"You got it."

Yes, she thought, pressing the off button on the receiver and placing it on the sink counter, she had it, all right. Looking at her reflection in the mirror, she traced the outline of her lips, the outline of Tony's mouth, with the tip of her finger.

Problem was, what exactly was "it" and what was she going to do about "it" once she found out?

She stood under the hot, pulsating water of the shower for a long time.

"Where is your mind, Tony?"

"Hmm?" Realizing that he'd been staring out the window instead of listening to his aunt, Tony had the decency to blush. As he turned to look at her, he gave her the most innocent expression he had. "Did you say something, Aunt Bridgette?"

Bridgette suppressed a laugh as she put the last of the baby food jars into the cupboard. It seemed as if each one of them had brought Tony a week's supply. They were gone now, taking with them the noise and the laughter. Only the overflow of their good intentions had remained behind in their wake.

She had chosen to remain behind a little while, knowing Tony would find it easier to ask her for help than the others. Wanting to assure herself that he would be all right before she, too, went home.

She'd been talking about Dottie's little bombshell when she'd realized that Tony had probably heard perhaps every tenth word.

"I said a great many 'somethings,' but you have not heard any of them." Closing the cupboard, she smiled knowingly at him. She'd mothered countless children, she knew the signs. "So, where do you know her from?"

"'Her'?"

"The woman who has stolen your thoughts." When he still gave no acknowledgment that he knew who she was talking about, Bridgette elaborated, even though she knew it wasn't necessary. "The little blond thing who was here."

"Work. I know her from work," he said, turning away from Bridgette. "She designed the high school we're building."

Bridgette knew all about Mikky, having garnered the information from the others. But she wanted to hear it from Tony, wanted to get him talking about the young woman with the pretty smile. Wanted to get him thinking even more about her than he apparently was. "Oh, she must be very smart, then."

Tony knew that tone, had heard it often enough when he was growing up. His aunt was up to something. Something that had to do with Mikky. He wanted to nip it in the bud before whatever it was got out of hand.

"Not so smart, Aunt Bridgette. She got a lot of things wrong with the design."

It was the first thing that came into his head. But it wasn't the design he was really thinking of. It was a soft female form that had no business occupying his mind.

Bridgette nodded thoughtfully. "And you—you will show her how to make them right, yes?"

As if it could ever be that easy. Feeling suddenly very drained, he sank down on the sofa. "I would if she listened once in a while instead of arguing."

Bridgette took a seat next to him, her eyes telling him that he had her full attention. "This Mikky, she argues with you?"

He laughed shortly. "I don't think she knows how not to argue."

Cocking her head like a little bird contemplating making breakfast out of the worm it saw before it, Bridgette appeared to think his observation over. "She seemed to be very agreeable to me, but then, I am only an old woman, not a handsome young man."

Coming from his aunt, the compliment embarrassed him. He shrugged it aside. "What I look like, or don't look like, doesn't have anything to do with it." And then he smiled at her. "And you're not an old woman." He brushed a kiss on her cheek. "You're a knockout."

The term brought forth a nostalgic smile as she remembered another voice telling her the exact same thing. "So your uncle Sal used to say." Bridgette patted his hand. "So, is she coming back, this smart young woman who likes to argue with you?"

He supposed that's why he kept glancing toward the window. Watching for her. Because he wanted her to return? Or because he didn't?

"I don't think so." Mikky had left over four hours ago, at the height of the bedlam. Hot and cold running children wherever he'd looked. "She probably thought I had all the help I needed."

Bridgette leaned forward, cupping his cheek affectionately. Once, when they had first gotten married, her Salvator had promised her a house resounding with the laughter of children. Because of medical complications, they could only have Angelo. Rather than bewail the cruel turn of fate, she and her husband had made up for it by opening their hearts to a legion of foster children and to her brother-in-law's motherless son. Tony was as much hers as the others were.

"This is true. You do. You will always have us." She allowed a pause. "But sometimes a person needs even more help than that. Leave yourself open to it, Tony. You won't regret it."

Tony knew what she was saying, knew she meant well. Knew, too, that it wasn't going to happen. Not for him. He wouldn't let it. Love was too much trouble and hurt too badly. He was satisfied with where he was. And that's where he would remain. Emotional desolation suited him. And it was preferable to pain.

The sound of the doorbell ringing just then, as if taking some heavenly cue, had her smiling. "Ah, there she is, back again."

"You're wrong." He crossed to the door, opening it. "She has better things to do than—"

Stunned, he stared at Mikky standing on the newly placed Welcome mat Dottie had insisted on making him accept. His first response was to look over his shoulder at his aunt.

"How did you do that?" he wanted to know.

Not waiting for an invitation, Mikky walked in. "Do

what?'' She looked to Bridgette for an answer, wondering whether she would like it once she received it.

Bridgette wore her triumph well, like a regal queen who knew the extent of her powers. "I told him you would be back."

Mikky could see why Tony had been surprised. *She* hadn't even known that she was going to return—until the restlessness had gotten too much to bear. It had urged her to her car and coaxed her to drive to Tony's apartment. She looked at Bridgette uncertainly. "How did you know that?"

Now that it had transpired, Bridgette could afford to downplay it. "It was easy." Taking Mikky's chin in her hand, Bridgette raised her head and turned it toward Tony to underscore her point. So that he could see, too. "You have kind eyes. Kind eyes mean a kind soul."

Against his will, Tony looked at Mikky's eyes. They weren't kind, they were bedeviling. And maybe just the slightest bit hypnotic.

He blew out an impatient breath. Right about now he could have used Justin's crying to rescue him from this. But for once the baby was silent. It figured. Where was a good set of lungs when you needed them?

"I think you're thinking of someone else, Aunt Bridgette."

Placing her hand on Mikky's forearm to ensure her attention, Bridgette leaned into her. "Be patient with him," she confided. "He is still, how do you say, a work in progress, yes?"

Mikky couldn't help laughing. That would sum Tony up to a T. "Yes."

Tony didn't particularly care for being the subject under discussion. "I'm not a work in progress. I'm finished." The moment the words were out, he glanced toward Mikky and had the uneasy feeling he'd just uttered a prophesy. "What *are* you doing here?"

But it was Bridgette, not Mikky, who answered his question. "That is simple, she knew your cousins would have to go home. That I would have to go home. And that you would refuse all of our offers to come stay with us. So she has returned to help you care for this good fortune, the Christmas baby the angels have brought your way. Understand?"

Where did he begin to unravel that? He went for the obvious. "It's not Christmas yet, Aunt Bridgette."

"Soon."

To prove her point, she waved at the little, decorated Christmas tree Dottie had brought with her. Although it was artificial, the spirit was still there. Frankie had decorated it for Tony. Alessandra had helped, when she hadn't been covertly staring at the young man as if he had just made the journey across the ocean from Hawaii to California on foot.

"And it is never too soon to give a Christmas gift, eh? It spreads the spirit." With what sounded like a stage sigh, Bridgette picked her purse up from the table. "I will be going now." But instead of going toward the door and leaving, she picked up Tony's hand and examined the fingers carefully.

Aware that Mikky was grinning broadly, he tried to pull his hand away. Bridgette did not release them. "What are you doing?"

"Checking to see that they are not broken. Good, you can use them for pressing buttons on the telephone." She set his hand free. "Remember, call me if you need anything." She looked at Mikky. "He is very stubborn."

"Tell me something I don't know."

Without missing a beat, Bridgette nodded. "All right, I will. He is a good man and worth the trouble." She looked at her nephew. "Eh, Tony?"

He wasn't entirely certain what was going on here, only that it was making him exceedingly uncomfortable. He indicated the window. Outside, dusk was beginning to finger the scenery.

"You'd better go before it gets dark."

"They worry about my eyes, he and the others." Bridgette crossed to the door, Mikky and Tony following her. "My eyes are fine. They see things he does not." She winked at Mikky. "But I go."

Bemused, Mikky turned from the door to look at Tony. She didn't know if the red tinge was due to annoyance or embarrassment, but she suspected a little bit of both. "I like her."

"Everyone does." He turned away. "She talks a little too much, though."

"I don't think so."

"That's because compared to you, Aunt Bridgette's a mute," Tony said, laughing.

"I didn't come here to argue."

"So why did you come?"

Why did you? a small voice asked. The same small voice that had asked the question before, as she'd been driving over here. She had no more answer now than she'd had before.

But she couldn't tell Tony that. Couldn't tell him that restlessness had propelled her here, because he might mistake her motives or make something more out of it than it was: a gesture of goodwill from one human being to another.

"Because I had a sudden vision of you trying to give Justin a bath and maybe accidentally drowning him."

It sounded lame to her, even though her tone was cloaked in bravado. She supposed that part of the reason she'd returned was because she couldn't get the image of Tony holding the baby out of her mind.

Seeing him like that told her a great deal more than his words did.

"A bath?" he repeated. "Why does he need a bath? He didn't go anywhere and every time he had his diaper changed, my aunt practically sterilized him. It's even money whether or not he'll ever be able to have kids of his own."

Mikky laughed. "I didn't think you had a sense of humor."

Tony bristled at what he took as a negative criticism. "Everyone's got a sense of humor." Shoving his hands into his front pockets, he wondered whether or not she expected him to offer her dinner or something. He supposed it would do no harm, especially since Justin was sleeping. There was suddenly enough food in his refrigerator now to see him through a month-long hibernation. "Not too much I find funny these days, that's all."

Mikky knew he was referring to the accident. Knew, too, that he had to get past it if he was ever going to live life again instead of just going through the motions. "There's humor in almost everything, you just have to look for it."

Before they could get into a debate on the matter, she looked around. The army of boxes was gone now, leaving a nicely decorated apartment in its wake. She wondered if the sofa, which hadn't been there before, was a donation or something Tony had allowed to be brought out of storage. There was a self-storage unit not far from where he lived.

"They did a pretty nice job," she enthused. There were a couple of paintings on the wall, a matching chair facing the sofa, and now that she thought of it, she didn't remember whether or not the TV set had been by the window earlier or not. The boxes had tended to overwhelm the field of vision.

"There's more room," he acknowledged carelessly.

Did the man ever show any kind of feelings besides anger?

"You know, it really wouldn't hurt you to agree with me once in a while." She heard Justin fussing in the next room. Showtime, she thought. "I promise not to hold it against you."

"Wouldn't want to set a precedent," Tony murmured. But there was something in her eyes that wouldn't let him just leave it at that. "All right," he allowed, "they did a nice job."

Amusement curved her mouth, but a victory was a victory, no matter how small. "There, was that so hard?"

"You'll never know."

"Probably not." She hooked her arms around one of his, leading him to the bedroom. "C'mon, let me give you your first lesson in how to bathe a baby."

In their largesse, it seemed that everyone had forgotten to bring a small tub for Justin. Tony thought that would put an end to it, but he realized he should have known better. This was Mikky. Nothing seemed to stop her once she made up her mind to do something.

"Mothers used kitchen sinks way before they came up with kiddie tubs."

"The sink?" He looked at her incredulously as he

followed her to the kitchen. She held Justin captive against her. "Like a dish?"

"Like a cute, messy little dish," Mikky cooed, talking to Justin.

It didn't surprise him that she talked all through the baby's bath, alternating between directing her words to him and to Justin. Justin at least seemed to enjoy the nonstop barrage that came his way. Tony, on the other hand, found it annoying. At least, that was what he told himself. It was easier feeling annoyed than feeling something else. Anything else.

The last thing he wanted was to see Mikky in a flattering light. He chalked it up to his sense of self-preservation.

Justin was bathed, changed and fed. Tony found himself lingering through all the stages, rather than going off to tackle the work he had brought home with him. Work that he turned toward as a way of numbing his mind so that the thoughts wouldn't come.

Watching Mikky with Justin aroused feelings within him he didn't feel he should have to deal with.

He left the room abruptly, leaving Mikky to wonder what it was she had said or done this time to set him off. Putting Justin down for the night in the portable crib that Angelo and Allison had brought, she tiptoed out of the room.

Half expecting to find herself alone in the apartment, she found Tony in the kitchen. The man was surrounded with bowls and pots. "You cook?"

"I'm Italian. It's in the genes. Besides, this isn't cooking, it's warming." He indicated the serving of shrimp scampi he'd just taken out. "Want some?"

Her smile was warm as she said, "I'd love some."

Sitting opposite him at the table, Mikky discovered

that if she wanted conversation, she had to initiate it herself and then keep it moving. Tony seemed perfectly content to eat in silence. Silence drove her crazy.

"So, I take it that you haven't heard anything about Justin's absent parents," she said.

By Tony's count she'd only been away a little more than four hours—not that he was counting, he told himself. Only that he'd happened to notice the time when she left. In any case, four hours was hardly time for any earth-shattering revelations to occur. There'd been no more notes from the baby's parent, no mysterious messages left on his phone at work or even here. It was as if Justin had been dropped out of the sky. Except that he hadn't.

He didn't even raise his eyes from his plate. "If I had, he wouldn't be here."

"True. Aren't you the least bit curious why you were singled out?"

"I wasn't singled out." Popping the top of a can of soda, he began pouring some for himself when he stopped abruptly and held the can out to her. She smiled, taking it from him and pouring a little for herself. "I just happened to be there."

Did he really believe that, or did it somehow keep him detached to think that? "So you think it was just the luck of the draw."

The shrug was dismissive. "No reason to think anything else."

She'd watched him earlier, after they'd given Justin his bath. In the space of less than a day, Tony seemed far more comfortable holding the baby. Certainly more than he had last night. He was getting the hang of it. More than that, she could see him getting used to this very quickly. Concern had her pointing out the obvious.

"You know, you can't keep him. He's not a puppy. If his parents don't turn up—"

Tony put down his fork, his mouth firm. "I already told you, I'll handle that when and if the time comes."

He was playing ostrich. She knew the danger in that. For years she'd secretly held on to the belief that her mother would return, that she couldn't have just walked away and left her. It brought a very bitter sense of betrayal when she'd finally accepted the truth.

"And, according to you, when will the time come? In a day? Two, three? A week? Eighteen years?"

"That was a hell of a jump." Annoyed, he got up from the table.

She was on her feet, following him into the next room. "No more than the one I think you're making in your mind."

He whirled around on his heel to glare down at her. "You have no idea what's on my mind. If you did, you might be dialing 911."

Mikky raised her chin defensively. "I wouldn't have to. One of my brothers is a cop."

"A cop." His dark eyebrows converged and narrowed. "You didn't call and tell him about this, did you?"

She couldn't lie. Didn't believe in it. Even so, her throat felt a little dry as she made the admission. "Off the record—"

"Off the record," he echoed, his voice rising. "Does that mean off his brain, too? He's a cop, Mikky. He's supposed to report things. Damn it, how could you?" he demanded. "What gives you the right to think you can interfere in my life?"

She didn't react well to being shouted at, especially since she'd done what she had for the best reasons.

Emotional to a fault, she wasn't always strictly driven by her emotions. The way he apparently was this time.

"I asked Thad—off the record," she ground out, "to see if there were any reports of missing or kidnapped babies."

He stared at her as if she'd just said she'd had her brother check the files for alien abductions. "Kidnapped?"

Obviously he hadn't even thought of that. "It's a possibility."

"Why would someone go through the trouble of kidnapping a baby and then leave it with me?"

There were a whole host of reasons. "Remorse, fear, second thoughts." She was going toe-to-toe with him now. "I don't know, I just wanted to cover all bases."

"They're *my* bases, and *you* don't have to cover them," he said, dragging his hand through his hair. "You've got a hell of an imagination, you know that?"

On the cusp of a fight, she was pugnacious now. "Yeah, I do. I find it an asset."

"An asset," he repeated, rolling the word around on his tongue. "Oh, you mean as in helping you create beautiful buildings that could only exist in that fanciful head of yours because they don't have a prayer of standing up in reality?"

They were back to the high school. If Marino wasn't so pigheaded and had an ounce of vision, he could see the possibilities. Both in the building and in his life. Mindful for the baby, Mikky struggled to curb her temper and keep her voice down.

She looked at him pointedly. "You make your own reality."

He met her glare head on. "I don't seem to be having much success in that."

She had no trouble understanding what he meant. "You want me to leave?"

"Yes." But as she turned away, he barked out, "No," and then growled, "damn it."

She was expressionless, her voice devoid of emotion. "I'm sorry, but I don't know how to do 'damn it.' Just what kind of command is it?"

"It's not a command, it's frustration. You're one hell of a confusing woman, you know that?"

There was enough electricity bouncing between them to light up San Francisco for a week. She gave up trying to ignore it. "Why, because you find yourself wanting to kiss me again?"

"Kiss you? I never said I wanted to kiss you again."

He didn't have to. "But you do, don't you?" Tony began to open his mouth, but she wasn't about to let him say anything yet. "It's okay, that kiss this morning knocked me for a loop, too. I was hoping you'd do it again so that I could see I was just being delusional before."

"Why would you have had to be delusional before?"

"Because nobody could have kissed like that."

Without knowing he was doing it, Tony took her into his arms. "Like what?"

"Like I could feel my hair grow."

How had she come to fit so snugly against him? "So you want to do this in the name of science?"

Her eyes were smiling, appearing to see right through him. "As good an excuse as any."

No, he thought as he brought his mouth down to hers, it wasn't.

Chapter Eight

It was the kind of kiss dreams were made of. Exciting, fiery. Tender.

But Tony didn't want to dream.

Lord help him, he couldn't seem to make himself want to wake up, either.

Not yet, just a little more, a voice within him pleaded. A second to remember, to feel, to know he hadn't become all steel and rock inside. That there was still something of the man who had been a husband and a father left.

Holding her closer to him, he let his lips roam over hers, absorbing the tantalizing, seductive flavor he found there. Who would ever have thought that someone whose tongue was so tart could taste so sweet?

Not him, that was for damn sure.

A man could get lost here, just savoring a feast. Just feeling like a man. With needs and passions and desires.

For Mikky it was like jumping out of the plane only to discover, at the worst possible time, that the parachute was still sitting tucked under the seat. A cry of excitement, of exhilaration throbbed within her, begging for release. But all sound had frozen in Mikky's throat.

And her lips were no help. They were otherwise occupied.

It was thrilling. It was frightening. And she had absolutely no idea where to go from here. Had no idea about anything at all, only that "here" was a wonderful place to be.

She felt her heart racing. But where was it racing to? Would there be anyone at the finish line once she got there?

Tony vaguely became aware that there was some sort of peripheral noise intruding into this hellish paradise he was trying to find his way through.

Crying.

Justin.

Justin was crying.

The realization brought reality back with it, driving a wedge between them. Startled, Tony pulled away, feeling as if he'd just been saved from going under for the third and final time.

Her knees were actually wobbly, Mikky thought, stunned by the discovery. So much for fluke reactions. She looked at Tony. "I think science just got burnt to a crisp."

Dazed, trying to reconcile the ringing in his ears with the whimpering he heard coming from his bedroom, Tony could only stare at her. "What?"

Mikky seriously doubted if she could get in a lungful of air without sounding as if she was gasping. What *had* he done to her?

"We were supposed to be doing that as an experiment, in the name of science, remember?" He was looking at her as if she'd just sprouted another head. "I said that science just got burnt to a crisp."

"Yeah. Whatever."

The best thing to do was just to retreat, to use Justin's crying as a diversion and hope that if he ignored it, the problem would go away. But *she* was the problem, and Tony damn well knew he could make book on the fact that she wasn't going away. Not unless he pushed her.

He turned around abruptly, bumping into her. It didn't surprise him that she was right behind him. He would have been surprised if she hadn't been. He had to stop this before it got way out of control.

"Look, something's happening here I don't want to happen." She was staring at him, staring at him with those eyes of hers. He had to look into them to get his point across. But it wasn't easy. "I loved my wife."

"I didn't realize that was being questioned."

"It's not." How had this even come about? All he wanted was to be left in peace for the rest of his life. Was that too much to ask? "I don't want another relationship."

"Not saying that we're about to have one," she qualified, "but I take it that means you want to play it safe."

"Yes. I want to play it safe." She was trying to make him feel like a coward, he thought. Whether he was or not was his business, not hers. Why did she think she had the right to keep butting in? What gave her the right to kiss him like that, to make him forget all his promises to himself? To make him, for the briefest moment, forget everything. "You got a problem with that?"

Mikky spread her arms wide, innocently. "Not if you don't." Something pushed her on to ask, "Were you happy with Teri?"

What kind of a question was that? Tony wondered. "Of course I was, what—"

There was no doubt in Mikky's mind now, that the wounds had gone deep. How far did he have to dig down before he could begin healing again? "Don't you like being happy?"

"Not if it comes with too high a price tag."

If everyone was like that, the world would have died out with Adam and Eve. "You know what they say, no pain, no gain."

"Then I guess I just won't gain," he said, his glance sweeping over her lips.

She knew it wasn't a battle to be won in an hour or day. This one, to be achieved, was going to take time. "Suit yourself." Justin's cries, unheeded, were becoming lusty in tone. As least Justin was a male she could handle.

"Where are you going?"

She thought he'd be able to figure that out on his own. She nodded toward the bedroom doors. "Justin's crying."

"I can take care of him myself."

The icy tone all but said, "you're dismissed." She didn't need to be on the receiving end of the bum's rush. Mikky turned around again to face Tony. Her tone was every bit as cold as Tony's. Two could play this deep-freeze game. "Then I guess there's no reason for me to stay any longer."

He looked past her head. "Guess not."

It didn't matter if his kiss could set paper on fire at ten paces. Some things just weren't worth the agony. "See you Monday."

"Not," he murmured as the door slammed in her wake, "if I see you first."

* * *

Upset and trying to find a place for the emotions that Tony had sent into an uproar, Mikky spent the remainder of the weekend cleaning and putting things in order. If they couldn't get organized in her head, the least she could do was organize her closets and drawers.

She concentrated on trying not to think about Tony and trying not to wait for the telephone to ring. When it invariably did, she knew before answering that it wouldn't be him. Tony wasn't about to call and apologize for behaving like the rear end of a horse. And if he needed any help in dealing with Justin, he had more than an army of helpful relatives to turn to.

He had no need of her.

She supposed she had difficulty believing and accepting that. But there were actually people in the world, she mocked herself as she swept out her garage, who got along perfectly well without her help.

With a sigh she leaned on her broom. Served her right for getting involved in the first place, she thought. Parking her broom against a wall, she went into the house to do something really constructive.

Mikky threw herself into the overwhelming-and-daunting project of trying to second-guess what part of her design Marino would attack next. Second-guessing how his mind worked wasn't easy on any level, but she was going to be as prepared as she could be, given the circumstances.

She fell asleep Sunday night over her drawing board.

Sleep was still fringing her eyes as she drove onto the vast, graded lot on Monday morning. Actually, it wasn't really even morning yet, she thought. She had to be crazy, coming here so early. And yet, staying home until a decent hour held no appeal, either. She might as well be working.

Thinking herself alone as she parked by her small trailer, she started as the flashlight shone into her car, breaking up the soothing dark.

"Oh, it's you, Ms. R." Sheepishly, the security guard flipped up his flashlight before turning it off. "I thought maybe it was some young punks, looking to make off with something."

Mikky got out, locking her door out of habit. "This is Bedford, Pete." She smiled at him to show no harm had been done even though the little white dot in front of her eyes was probably going to continue flittering in and out for the next fifteen minutes or so. "We're not zoned for punks, young or otherwise."

A solid, older man, Pete Reynolds pushed back the brim of his gray cap with the tip of his thumb.

"Sure beats some of the other places Max and I have guarded. Thing I have to be most careful about on this assignment is not falling asleep." He laughed to himself as he followed her to the steps of her trailer. "Not like that time I had to guard a construction site in East L.A. Plenty of action there. Had the cops out more than once."

She nodded, preoccupied but trying to be polite. "Well, you won't get that here." As a thought occurred to her, she looked at the security guard. Brought in on the first day, he was on the site every night, dusk to dawn. It was company policy. There always had to be a guard around to make sure that none of the materials were stolen.

Which meant he had been here Friday night.

She remembered seeing him now. "Pete, you didn't see anything suspicious Friday evening, did you?"

"Suspicious?" Very dark eyebrows pulled together as he concentrated. "How do you mean?"

She was certain the guard would have investigated if he'd noticed something out of the ordinary, but it never hurt to ask, just in case. "Somebody carrying something. Leaving a baby on the steps of Marino's trailer."

Warm, chocolate-brown eyes looked at her incredulously. "A baby? Somebody left a baby? When?"

"Friday evening. Around six." She could see by his expression that he had no idea what she was talking about. So much for getting lucky. "Never mind, I just took a shot."

His expression was contrite, as if he was very sorry to disappoint her.

"I must have been on the other side of the site when that happened. I patrol the grounds once an hour." Pete scratched the German shepherd he kept on a tight leash behind the ear. "Keeps me and Max alert."

Mikky flipped through her keys, looking for the one to the trailer. She nodded at his explanation. "Sorry to bother you."

"Hey, no bother." He began to turn away, then stopped, curiosity getting the better of him. "What happened to the baby?"

Finding the right key, she inserted it into the lock and opened the door. "Well, it looks like Mr. Marino's temporarily taken custody of him." She saw genuine interest in the older man's eyes. "He thinks the mother is coming back."

Pete considered her words. "Doesn't usually happen." Sighing, he shook his head. Sensing something was wrong, the dog drew closer to his master. "What's he going to do if she doesn't show?"

It seemed everyone acknowledged that possibility but Marino. "He hasn't thought that far yet."

A philosophical, mild smile tugged on the guard's lips. "He seems like a good guy, Mr. Marino. I'm sure he'll come up with something."

She certainly hoped that he was right in this case. Mikky opened her door. "I'll see you later, Pete. Max." She nodded at the twosome.

"Sorry I couldn't be more help," Pete called in after her.

"Not your fault."

And not, she reminded herself as she closed the door behind her, *your problem.*

The first order of business was getting coffee into her veins.

Mikky was on her second cup of mudlike coffee when she heard the knock on her door. Wondering if the troops had landed and she was about to be invaded, she sidled past the table that took up most of the available space in the narrow trailer and crossed to the door. She felt her adrenaline starting up.

As a rule the crew didn't come looking for her. The men were pleasant enough to her, but Marino kept them hopping, which left little time for her to get to know any of them, and technically she wasn't part of what was going on. Supposedly, she had done her part, and her presence was an intrusion. At least, that was what Marino made her feel.

Damn, why couldn't the man kiss like a frog? Wasn't it bad enough that he looked like a fairy-tale prince, did he have to kiss like one, too?

With a barely suppressed huff, she pulled open the door.

The fairy-tale prince was on her doorstep. The prince-in-waiting was tucked under his arm.

Mikky looked from Tony to Justin. The former wore a faint scowl, the latter a sunny smile. It was obvious that Marino could learn something from his foundling.

Still, she was surprised to see the baby. "You brought Justin with you?"

"I thought you might be more forgiving if I had a baby in my arms."

Suspicion piqued as she reached for Justin. Tony surrendered the boy after a beat. "Forgiving?"

Was she going to make him spell it out? Apparently so, he thought grudgingly. "About Saturday night. I meant what I said about getting involved." With every word, Tony's tongue was getting thicker. He wasn't any good at this kind of thing. Never needed to do this until he'd met her. Now he seemed to be doing it all the time. "But maybe I could have said it better. It was no excuse to behave like a...a—"

"Jerk. Ass. Clod." With each suggested label, her smile grew.

Well, this had certainly been a bad idea, thought Tony. "I don't need a thesaurus."

"Just trying to be helpful." Her grin swept right through him even though he tried to prevent its entry. She turned her attention to the baby. "Hi-ya, Justin." With a laugh, she nuzzled him. Tony couldn't help thinking how natural she looked, holding Justin like that. Another time, another place...

Mikky raised her eyes to his. "You didn't really bring Justin here with you as a visual aid, did you?"

He shrugged his reply to the implication in her question. "That and because I thought that maybe if he was here, someone on the site might recognize him—or have regrets."

Mikky couldn't decide if he was hoping to succeed or fail. The longer it took to find Justin's errant mother, the longer Tony got to keep the boy.

She turned her attention to something far less serious. "Where did you get the hard hat?" She tapped the white helmet with her finger, catching Justin's attention. Giggling, he grabbed her finger and held on.

Just like he had a hold of her heart, she realized. It didn't take long with kids.

"Angelo gave it to me." Tony had taken Justin over with him to his aunt Bridgette's for her mandatory Sunday dinner and had spent part of the time explaining to her why Mikky hadn't come with him. But that wasn't something he wanted Mikky to know. "He has several for when he brings his kids onto a site."

Justin had his fingers firmly around the brim. Mikky carefully pried them off. "You look very dashing, Justin."

Not unlike your keeper, she added silently.

"So now what?" she asked.

"I thought maybe you could watch him for a while. I forgot I have to meet with a supplier this morning and—"

She put him out of his misery. "Sure. Justin and I will go over my blueprints together, won't we, Justin?"

The boy gurgled.

"See, he's a lot more agreeable than you are already," she said.

"That's because he's too young to know what he's letting himself in for." But Tony was smiling as he said it.

* * *

Justin, Mikky noted later that morning, attracted attention like a magnet dropped into a box of metal filings. The gorgeous weather had prompted Mikky to bring Justin out of the trailer to enjoy the day. That, and Tony's idea that someone might recognize the little boy.

No one seemed to recognize him, but that didn't stop people from coming over. Weather-beaten, hard-edged men were transformed into malleable wads of mush when taking turns clustering around the sweet-tempered baby. Everyone, it appeared, wanted to hold Justin.

Even the security guard had taken his turn, entertaining Justin with his keys. The foreman, a heavyset man named Mendoza, was a natural with Justin. He had five kids and a grandchild on the way, courtesy of his second oldest.

"It's gonna be a boy," Mendoza told Mikky as they queued up to the lunch truck. "They already know." It was obvious he didn't think much of the idea of finding out ahead of time. "In my day you waited to find out what it was going to be. Nobody likes surprises anymore. Me, I kinda think you lose something that way." He shifted Justin so that the boy was facing him. "How about you, little guy?"

Justin responded with a toothy grin as he drooled down the front of Mendoza's jacket.

"Here, you've hogged the kid long enough, give him to me," a riveter with a tattoo of a cobra on his hand said, reaching for Justin.

The crane operator nudged him out of the way. "I've had lunch. I can hold him."

Mikky looked at Tony, who'd only now joined her. "If we charge everyone for a turn, we could start up a nice college fund for him."

Tony muttered something she didn't catch as he elbowed his way through the crowd. "I'll take him." Without waiting for a comment, Tony took the boy into his arms. "It's time he had something to eat."

"Sure, boss. He's all yours." Mendoza surrendered the baby to him.

"I'm impressed," Mikky told Tony, falling into step beside him.

Justin's cheeks were bright red. He'd had enough of an outing for now, Tony thought. "I wasn't aware I was saying anything impressive."

How much of that brusqueness was an act and how much was genuine? Mikky had watched him with Justin, and she knew there was a warmer side to Tony. Why did he insist on being such a bear around her? "You remembered his feeding time."

"I eat, he eats, no big deal." Tony stopped at the door of his trailer, his fingers on the knob. Escape was within his reach, but for some reason he didn't feel like taking hold of it. Instead, he glanced at Mikky. "You can join us if you want."

"Ah, a warm invitation. How can I resist?"

He frowned, walking in. "Does everything have to be a crack with you?"

"I dunno." She pretended to think it over. "Does everything have to be offhand with you? An offhand invitation, an offhand apology…"

Shifting Justin to his other side, he held up a hand. He'd already learned that if he didn't stop her, she'd be off and running with no end in sight.

"Okay, point taken. If you have no better offers, would you do me the extreme honor of dining in my trailer with Justin and me?"

"Better." She grinned at him. "And I've never had

a better offer." She looked around the trailer. "Did you bring his food with you?"

He pointed to a large tote bag that Shad's wife had lent him. "Right there."

Mikky opened up the bag. Inside was a complete array of everything Justin would need to get through the day. She looked at him in surprise. "Who packed this for you?"

"I did," he informed her. "It took a while, but it's coming back to me."

"Did you take your own son on outings?"

"Yeah." The desire to be curt and cut her off flared and disappeared as the memory of his son chased it away. "Yeah, I did." He turned her around. "So do I pass inspection?"

Mikky took out a jar of rice and turkey dinner. "You don't need me to validate that."

"Just so you know."

While she fed Justin, he unwrapped the sandwiches they'd gotten at the truck and placed them on the desk. Two cans of soda completed the setting. "I can do that, you know."

"I know." She smiled at him. "We'll take turns."

Was it him, or was there something kinder about that smile? As if she had his number but wasn't going to use it. Just yet.

Sitting down opposite her, Tony picked up his pastrami sandwich. Hungry earlier, he found that his appetite had mysteriously faded. Had to be the company. He set the sandwich down again, content to sip his soda and watch her feed Justin.

The domesticity of the scene soothed him. There was a danger in allowing himself to get too comfortable with this. With her. "You haven't heard anything from your brother, have you?"

"Not a word." She'd only called the one time and then decided that no news was good news. "Anyone here look as if they might be feeling guilty to you?"

He shook his head. Although, if he were being truthful, he would have to admit that he hadn't really been looking, despite what he'd told her.

"Not so far as I can see." He leaned over to wipe Justin's mouth when an abundance of apple sauce threatened to burble out his lips. "I'm beginning to think that it was someone driving by who just happened to see the site and left Justin here on impulse."

Scraping the bottom of the jar, she fed Justin the last bit of apple sauce. "You might be right. At least, Pete said he didn't see anyone."

He looked at her blankly. "Pete?" He didn't remember any of the crew being named that, but then, he could be wrong.

"The security guard." She wiped Justin's chin and tossed the towel aside. "Don't you know his name?"

"I'm not very good with names. Truth is, I'm not very good with people. Not anymore, anyway." He took Justin from her, freeing her hands. "Go ahead, eat your sandwich."

She smiled. He was coming along. For however long Justin was in his life, the little boy was a positive influence. "It's like riding a bike. It'll come back to you." Draining her own soda, she set it down, then eyed his. Mikky raised a brow, looking at him.

He gestured toward the can. "Go ahead."

Mikky took a sip from his can. She had no idea why that felt so intimate, but it did. "I've had a chance to go over my design again.'' She waited for him to say something flippant.

''Mendoza said there was a light on in your trailer when he got here at six-thirty.''

''I got in at six.''

''Why?''

''I like to tackle things early.'' Mikky made her way into the minefield cautiously, waiting for the first explosion. ''When you have a chance, I'd like to discuss that point you raised on Friday—'' She was now fully armed to show him, in the politest way she knew how, exactly why she was right and he was wrong.

Busy playing with Justin, he waved away her words. ''No need, you were right.''

Mikky felt her jaw grow slack. She'd put in several hours on this. ''Excuse me?''

''The augmentation you showed me, it works.'' After he'd returned from Bridgette's on Sunday, Tony had taken a second look at what Mikky had proposed. In a more tolerant frame of mind, he'd realized that her suggestion solved the potential stress problem he'd initially detected. ''I should have seen it. The design's a little futuristic, but it's doable.'' He stopped. Still seated opposite him, Mikky was looking all around the trailer. ''What are you looking for?''

''A pod.''

He picked up on the science fiction reference. ''No pod, no invasion of the body snatchers. I took a closer look, that's all.''

''All'' wouldn't have been the way she would have put it. She smiled at him. ''Someone should have left a baby on your doorstep a long time ago.''

''Justin has nothing to do with it.''

She knew better. ''Whatever you say.''

Chapter Nine

Justin became the crew's mascot.

It happened quickly, effortlessly, taking hold in less than a couple of days. Tony took to bringing the boy with him every day. By the third day, Justin was a fixture on the site. Everyone took turns watching Justin, especially Mikky.

For Tony the bonding was even faster. It seemed to him that he and the sunny-faced little boy had taken to each other the moment he had picked him up from his doorstep. The effects generated by Justin's presence in his life were not isolated solely to his interaction with the baby. The darkness that had such an iron grip around Tony's world began to allow glimmers of light in.

Which, he decided later when he looked back, was probably how Mikky managed to seep in—through the fissures and the microscopic spaces that were emerging in the walls he'd kept around himself.

Justin was their catalyst, his and Mikky's.

Because of Justin, Tony noticed that their working relationship transformed into something other than open warfare. Tony's admission that perhaps he'd been too hasty dismissing aspects of her design paved the way to a better rapport between them.

Which paved the way for other things.

Granted, it had cost him to admit he was wrong. But to Tony's surprise, he had gained far more than he'd lost with that one simple action.

He'd gained Mikky as a friend. Beyond that, he wouldn't, couldn't, allow his thoughts to go. The territory out there was raw and hard to negotiate. He was still hurting.

But even so, Tony had to admit that there were more pluses to the woman than minuses. Once he stopped seeing her as a major annoyance, he realized that she was easier to work with than he'd initially thought. Like two halves of a whole, they complemented each other.

She had vision while he was practical. Rather than butt heads and shout, upsetting Justin, they strove to remain calm and reach for compromises.

Justin was their tranquilizer—and so much more than that.

"A happy pill, that's what you are," Mikky told the baby as she changed him on the table that had previously held only blueprints. There was a container of baby powder on it now and a box of baby wipes. A half-empty plastic bag of diapers was nestled in the corner of the trailer, beside a minirefrigerator that housed his food. "You've had a positively calming effect on that man." Closing the diaper tabs, she tucked Justin's rompers back on, then picked him up in her arms. It was only two short weeks since he'd come into both their lives, and she felt as if she'd held the little boy in her arms forever.

She felt as if he were hers.

Don't go there, she warned herself.

It was bad enough that Tony had become so attached to the boy. She couldn't allow herself that luxury. She had no claim to Justin at all. But there was no denying that he had one on her. On her heart.

A little like, she mused, the big lug who took care of him.

Mikky raised Justin high overhead. Sweet, childish laughter surrounded her as he enjoyed his impromptu flight. "If we could bottle you, we'd make a fortune, you know that?"

"And if you could talk, Justin, you'd tell her that all she had to do was behave civilly and she would have gotten the same results." The door shut, punctuating Tony's words.

Mikky glanced over her shoulder, not all that surprised to see Tony standing behind her. It was an unspoken understanding that he could drop by whenever she had Justin in her trailer, and she could walk into his anytime Justin was with him. They had become, without ever putting it into words, each other's support group.

The feeling leeched out to areas beyond Justin, though that, too, was unspoken, but for very different reasons.

Mikky turned her attention back to the baby. "Can you say *bull,* Justin?"

Her trailer was smaller than his. Tony had difficulty maneuvering without bumping into something. This time it was Mikky he brushed up against as he went to retrieve Justin from her.

"Teaching him how to rebel already?" A warmth fingered him as he enfolded Justin in his arms. "How're you doing, big guy?"

"Teaching him how to wade through the muck and see the truth," she countered. Who would have thought that this was the same man she'd met three months ago in the mayor's office? Two weeks in Justin's company and he had gone through a remarkable transformation. "Face it, he's turned you into a human being."

Tony eyed her. "Meaning I wasn't before he came along?"

She couldn't help the smile that curved her mouth. Maybe being around Justin had changed her, as well. Not that long ago she would have answered Tony's question with a biting barb. Now she had no desire to match wits with him. "You know the answer to that yourself."

It was a crisp, sunny day, and he didn't feel like waltzing on the cusp of a disagreement. Some of the anger that had been his unshakable, steadfast companion had begun to slip away.

He changed the subject. "The project's coming along nicely. Looks as if we're going to be finished before deadline."

He'd sweated that a few times in the beginning, when they were afraid the supplies would be held up. But now everything was a go. The grading along the three acres where the school was to stand had all been completed, the foundation laid and now the actual construction was well underway. Everyone seemed to be working at maximum potential. Barring any unforseeable major mishaps, the late-deadline penalty no longer hung over their collective heads as an ever-present threat. There might even be a bonus in it for completing the job before deadline.

Mikky had monitored the crew's progress and thrilled as her design became more than lines on paper and a three-dimensional drawing on her computer screen. It was well on its way to becoming a reality. She'd had buildings she designed go up before, and the thrill had never left her. But this one was her first beneath her own banner. It was very special to her.

But the progress, something she had longed for earlier, now had a bittersweet component to it. The faster things went, the faster she would leave.

"I know." She blew out a breath, then turned away so he couldn't see the look in her eyes. "Looks as though I'll be packing up and leaving by the end of next week."

He'd forgotten about that. Because the design was working out so well now, there would be no need of her presence on the site soon.

"You're leaving during the hiatus?" Because things were ahead of schedule, the company could afford to knock off during the week between Christmas and New Year's.

She nodded. "Now that my plans are no longer in jeopardy of being trashed—" she looked at him significantly "—I can move on. I've got another project lined up."

And two more after that, hopefully. Her designs for both had already been submitted, and she was just waiting for the final verdicts to come in.

He glanced at the calendar on the wall. An elf trying to dig out a snowbound reindeer hovered over the dates. Christmas Eve was approaching quickly. "So Justin and I only have to put up with you for another week?"

Mikky inclined her head. "Looks like." Was he happy about that? Happy that he wouldn't be seeing her again? She didn't think she really wanted an answer. Not if it was the wrong one.

"Busy on Sunday?" he asked before he could think better of it and stop himself.

She didn't even have to think. "No more than usual." "Usual" entailed doing laundry and catching up with her life. This week that meant wrapping presents. Mikky cocked her head, studying him. Frustrated, she couldn't read anything in his expression. The man could play poker with the best of them. "Why, what did you have in mind?"

"Nothing." No, that was as far from the truth as day was from night. Tony had plenty on his mind, some things that he fervently wished he didn't.

She was turning away, and he knew that he was better off letting her go. But then he heard himself saying, "Aunt Bridgette cooks a big dinner every Sunday."

Clearing away the wet diaper, she restored her desk to order. Or some reasonable facsimile thereof. "So I heard."

He sighed loudly. "She likes the family to gather."

"Nice tradition." Mikky hunted up her set of pens. If he was taking Justin, then maybe she could get a little work done on the house that had been haunting her mind. She had no developer on tap yet, just an idea that refused to leave her alone.

Tony could tell she wasn't going to make this easy. He'd been half hoping that if he gave her her lead, she'd invite herself over. After all, that was her style, but suddenly, middance, she'd changed tempo. It figured.

He pushed the envelope a little further toward her.

"She likes keeping an extra place set for anyone who might drop by."

Mikky raised her eyes to his innocently. "Very considerate of her."

He strove to hang on to his patience. Even when the woman was being nice, she found a way to do it that irritated him. Shifting Justin to his other side, he moved closer to Mikky, trying to corner her undivided attention. "Would you like to drop by?"

She set down her oversize pad. "Not without an invitation."

"From her?"

Mikky brushed past him to the refrigerator to get a can of soda. "Or a designated representative."

It took only three steps to be next to her again. "All right, damn it, would you like to come?"

Popping the top, she took a long sip of the soda before looking at him. Her eyes were dancing. "You know, I have no idea why the U.N. hasn't already come by and scooped you up for their diplomatic corps. You just exude charm all over the place."

She'd been stringing him along. Why couldn't he find it in him to get angry and rescind the invitation? "I do, just not around you."

The laugh told him that she'd believe it when she saw it. "Why is that, do you think?"

Damn it, he should never have given in. Some impulses were meant to be ignored. Like the very strong one he had now—to kiss her just to shut her up.

And to taste her mouth again.

He pretended to be preoccupied with Justin's shoelace. "Like you said, we rub each other the wrong way."

They did, Mikky thought, but the key word here was

rubbed. It was the constant contact that was getting to both of them. "And yet you're asking me to dinner on Sunday."

"Family dinner," he emphasized. "And you can come or not, it's all the same to me."

With a laugh Mikky patted his cheek. He drew his head back. But not too quickly. "You make it hard to resist. Where and when?"

Tony gave her the particulars, then left. Striding back to his trailer, he told Justin that he really needed to have his head examined.

Trouble was he knew it hadn't been his head that had prompted him to invite her in the first place.

Sunday dinner at Bridgette's was served at five, but guests were required to arrive by two or earlier. Tony had decided to arrive late to spend as little time as possible with Mikky.

Instead, he arrived early and spent more than half the time slanting covert glances toward the door.

"You are expecting someone?" Bridgette finally asked him innocently after observing his behavior for over an hour.

"Um..."

How did he answer that without making it seem more than it was? Without letting his aunt make more of it than it was? Aunt Bridgette was the kindest woman in the world, but she had a tendency to want to see the entire world in terms of couples. Even couples who had no business being together.

The single unintelligible sound coming out of his mouth told Bridgette all she needed to know, confirming all her suspicions. Pleased, she picked up another potato and began peeling it quickly.

"Don't worry, if you asked her, she will come. Now, why don't you make yourself useful? Your cousins have finally stopped fighting over who's to be the straw boss of this thing and have put up the tree. Why don't you go over and help them decorate the tree? You're of no use to me in the kitchen." She took away the knife and potato he had been holding on to for the past five minutes.

He wasn't sure if he wanted to be out there with the others. Although Aunt Bridgette had a matchmaking bent, she knew how to keep her questions veiled. His cousins had never acquired that skill.

"I don't—"

Bridgette gave him a look that would have caused five-star generals to rush to obey. "That wasn't a suggestion, Tony. Go."

Saluting, he got off the stool. "Yes, ma'am." He felt her eyes on his back as he walked out of the kitchen.

He had dreaded the approach of Christmas, dreaded facing it alone with its memories of seasons past. Even in the midst of his family, he felt alone. There were things that lingered in his mind, haunting him. A certain word, a certain tune. So many things to bring to mind what he no longer had.

But now the dread had begun to dissipate, as if by magic. Things were different. There was Justin to care for and other things to take his attention away from his once-all-consuming hurt.

Shoving his hands into his pockets, he walked into the family room. It was amazing how much activity could be shoved into a relatively small room. When he built this house, Salvator had purposely made the ceilings in the living room and family rooms vaulted to give the house an open, airy effect—and to accommodate the ten-foot Christmas trees he foresaw standing there during the holidays.

The tree his cousins had chosen had come in just shy of eleven feet, necessitating a little surgery before it could wear its crown—a circle of three angels holding hands. Bridgette said each of the angels represented one of her children.

What space the tree didn't take up, his cousins and their children did, all getting in each other's way as they scrambled for lights, garlands and decorations.

Tony took in the joyful madness, shaking his head. "It's a wonder you guys ever build anything if you have this much trouble decorating a Christmas tree."

He glanced at the door, wondering if that was the doorbell he'd heard or if it was just his imagination.

Balancing on the next-to-the-top rung of the ladder, Angelo gave him a condescending look. "You gonna stand there, growing into the rug and criticizing, or are you going to help?"

"He'll help, right, Tony?" Without waiting for a reply, Alessandra put a string of lights into his hands. The top of her head brushed against his shoulder. The last time he'd been home for a visit, she had been a gangly fourteen, no longer a child and miles away from being a woman. The miles, he noticed, had melted away.

"You've become as bossy as Aunt Bridgette," he murmured.

Alessandra laughed, delighted. He couldn't have given her a more treasured compliment. There was no blood between her and her stepmother's foster mother. But Al felt that Bridgette Marino was as much her grandmother as Louisa, her late mother's mother was. More, because Bridgette was always there to talk to, to dispense love and wisdom along with batches of pignolia cookies that always seemed to just be coming fresh from the oven.

Of late, Al had cut back on the cookies, although not the supply of love and wisdom. A girl had to watch her figure when she had an eye on catching a certain some-one's attention.

That *was* the doorbell. Tony looked impatiently over his shoulder. Didn't anyone else hear it?

"Isn't somebody going to answer that?" he asked irritably.

"You're somebody, right?" On the floor, testing an-other tangled line, Shad looked up at him. "We figured you'd let her in."

Tony'd almost taken a step to the door before the full impact hit him. He looked at Shad. "What makes you think that I'm—"

"Yeah, yeah." Two hands at the center of his back, Dottie pushed her cousin in the direction of the front door. "Just let the poor woman in before she comes to her senses, gets back into her car and drives for the county line."

"She's already circled the block twice," Frankie an-nounced from the living room.

Over by the playpen, Dottie frowned. They all took up a great deal of the available parking spaces. "Look-ing for a spot?"

"Looking for courage would be my guess," Allison interjected. She knew what it was like, facing this warm, exuberant family on their own territory. A little over-whelming at first. She'd been leery of it herself, but then, she'd never encountered family warmth to this de-gree before. Or any degree for that matter. Raised as an only child by a succession of nannies, she had a father who had thought that showing affection was a capital offense that only made the recipient the weaker for it. The Marinos and McClellans had taken some getting used to.

But it had been well worth it.

Muttering something unintelligible under his breath about the burden of having a family who never minded its own business, Tony went to answer the door.

"Hi." Feeling uncustomarily awkward, Mikky held up the bottle of wine she'd impulsively purchased an hour ago, after passing up a cake at a bakery. She'd been afraid that Bridgette might take it as an insult to her culinary abilities. Mikky felt pretty confident that the woman didn't make her own wine. "I didn't know what to bring."

Before he had a chance to take the bottle from her, Bridgette was at his elbow, gently nudging him aside. "Just yourself would have been enough." She took the wine, glancing at the label. Expensive. It meant the young woman was nervous. Good. "Come, it's cold outside."

It was a typical Southern California winter's day. The air was crisp, the sun warm. "Aunt Bridge, she works in construction," Tony protested. Besides, Mikky wasn't some fragile, hothouse flower in need of protection. Mikky struck him as a woman who would promptly knock anyone's block off who even remotely suggested she needed protecting.

To his surprise Mikky smiled her agreement.

That cinched it. He hadn't a clue how to read people. He was better off keeping company with Justin.

"Don't tempt fate," Bridgette admonished him. "Not over small things, anyway."

He had no idea what she was talking about and

wasn't about to ask. He figured it was a lot safer that way for everyone.

"Come say hello to everyone." Making good on her instruction, Bridgette took Mikky's arm and ushered her into the family room. A cacophony of hellos came sailing her way. "Then pick your task."

Mikky looked at her, puzzled. "My task?"

"Nobody eats without working today. You can help me in the kitchen." She gestured toward the room beyond. "Or help them decorate the tree." Bridgette glanced toward her nephew. "Tony, as you can see, has taken the part of the wooden Indian."

"It's Native American now, Ma," Angelo corrected her as he patiently worked out the knots in the string bunched up before him. He slanted a look toward his sons, playing beside Dottie. "You guys didn't play jump rope with this, did you?"

Three towheads vigorously shook their denial.

Bridgette shrugged. "Wooden person," she amended with a smart nod of her head, calling an end to it. "We are all people before someone decides to put us into categories."

It was hard to tell where one person started and another ended in this tangle of decorations, people and tree. Mikky looked around. "Where's Justin?" Was the baby sleeping through all this commotion? And how could they hear him if he cried?

"Supervising," Bridgette pointed toward the wide playpen on the floor. "You'll pick decorating the tree," Bridgette announced to Mikky.

Amused now, Mikky said, "I thought I was supposed to choose."

Bridgette was already on her way back to the kitchen. "You were taking too long to make up your mind."

"She tends to steamroll over people sometimes," Dottie told Mikky, open affection in her voice. Getting up from the floor, she dusted her jeans off. "God comes by for advice every Monday morning."

Shea leaned over his wife, brushed a kiss to her lips before getting back to the string of lights he'd been presented. "She passed that trait on."

Mikky rocked slightly on the balls of her feet. She looked around, trying to determine who was in charge now that Bridgette had left the room. "So, what do you want me to do?"

Shad looked at Angelo. Tony noticed the grin that passed between them. Now what?

Slipping his arm around Mikky, Shad drew her aside to the table where all the various decorations had been meticulously laid out. "Why don't you put hooks on the decorations?"

Seemed simple enough. Mikky glanced around. "Where're the hooks?"

Shad looked thunderstruck, then embarrassed, neither managed very convincingly. "That's right, we haven't brought them up yet. They're still in the storage cellar." He turned around to look at his cousin. "Why don't you go show her where the storage cellar is, Tony?"

Basements and attics were not part of the buildings that went up in Southern California. Intrigued, Mikky looked at Shad. "You have a storage cellar?"

"Doubles as a wine cellar," Angelo told her. With triumph, he set aside one untangled string, then sighed when his wife handed him another one. "Dad came from back East. Always missed having a basement. The cellar was his way of compromising."

"C'mon," Tony muttered. "Let me show you."

He led the way to the back stairs and then went down

ahead of her. Following, Mikky stood on the steps behind him, waiting until he opened the door.

The space was cramped. The light he turned on only made it look that much smaller and eerier.

Wondering if he was being quiet because he was embarrassed, Mikky tried to put him at ease. "Could they have been more obvious?"

At least she was being a good sport about it, Tony thought. Some of this was at her expense, too. "Not unless they hung a sign out saying Quiet, Matchmaking in Progress." He looked around, trying to remember where his aunt usually stored the decorations.

Mikky ran her hands along her arms. The cellar was chilly. "Too bad they don't know about our agreement not to get involved. They could have saved themselves a lot of needless planning."

He turned around, brushing against her. He hadn't realized that she was standing so close behind him. But he should have. "Yeah, too bad."

And too bad, he thought, that he didn't take it to heart himself.

Glancing up, he saw it. Small and pale green, it was festively decorated with a red ribbon. And hanging just over her head. "Mikky?"

She turned around in the tight corner, the tips of her short hair brushing against his chin. Just enough to arouse him. Just enough to make him want exactly what he'd told himself he didn't want.

"What?"

He pointed toward the low ceiling. "Somebody put up a sprig of mistletoe here." It wasn't much of a stretch to figure out who.

Mikky raised her eyes to look at it. "You know,"

she murmured softly, "I hear it's bad luck to go against tradition."

Why did she have to fit so well against him? And why was his resolve breaking apart so easily? He'd made his peace with the world the way it was, and now it was being thrown into chaos again.

But it was such tempting chaos. "Where did you hear that?"

Mikky couldn't take her eyes off his. Anticipation sent tiny electrical currents charging all through her. "Some place."

"Oh."

You would think that a man his age would have built up more willpower by now.

But he hadn't, Tony realized.

So he stood there, in the center of his aunt's storage cellar, having a ridiculous conversation with a woman he was having an increasingly great amount of difficulty getting out of his mind. Wanting her badly. It was a good thing she would be leaving soon. Before he wound up doing something really stupid. Something he would regret. "Wouldn't want any bad luck hitting the site."

Very slowly she moved her head from side to side. "Nope."

He framed her face with his hands, tilting it up toward his. Telling himself to go. Now. "Guess this means I have to kiss you."

"Guess so," she barely whispered.

Resistance is futile.

The sentence, uttered by a robotic, conquering race in one of his all-time favorite series, throbbed in Tony's brain like a mantra. No doubt about it, the creatures must have been thinking of Mikky when they coined the phrase.

Like a man who has had a vision of his own doom, Tony lowered his mouth to hers.

And felt the world explode.

Chapter Ten

No doubt about it, her eyelashes were definitely singed. Maybe even the roots of her hair. Feeling dazed, disoriented and equal parts contented and aroused, Mikky drew her mouth slowly away from his. For a man who was trying to keep his emotional distance, he certainly leaped over the chasm he'd created every time he kissed her.

A woman could easily get hooked on this. Mikky took a deep breath before she attempted to say anything coherent. "I don't know about you, but that's one tradition I think the world should really keep."

What was wrong with him? Tony wondered. Why did his willpower turn to dust every time he was close to her? This wasn't fair to either one of them and he didn't want to lead her on.

He didn't want to lead himself on.

"Mikky."

"Shh." She placed her fingertips to his lips to still them. "Don't spoil it with any disclaimers." Mikky tried very hard to ignore the affection that was flooding through her veins. She couldn't allow it to distract her and color the way things were. "I'm not asking you for anything, just to enjoy the moment. Nothing else, just that." She slid her fingers from his lips, gently feathering them along his mouth as she withdrew. "Okay?"

"Okay."

But was it? Was it okay? Tony didn't know.

He'd never expected to feel anything for anyone at all. Teri coming into his life had been an exciting surprise, one that, once he'd gotten his bearings, he'd embraced with enthusiasm. But after her sudden death, he'd sworn that he would never invest any of himself like that again.

He would have sworn he would never be able to.

Yet here he was, taking in a child, feeling things for a woman...setting himself up all over again. But this time he knew about the fall. Knew about it and, more than anything in the world, didn't want to experience it again. Because this time he wouldn't recover.

And yet...

He drew away from her, wishing that his uncle had built the cellar just a little larger.

Had it been St. Patrick's Cathedral, it still wouldn't have been big enough, he realized. "C'mon, we'd better find those hooks before they send a search party looking for us."

"I have a sneaking suspicion that won't be for a very long time." Her eyes indicated the small, suspended sprig above their heads. "Unless, of course, they usually hang mistletoe in the storage cellar."

He tried to shrug it off philosophically. Their intent had been good, he supposed. "My family thinks I should cheer up."

And he minded them butting in, Mikky thought. Nothing unusual about that.

"Families have a way of worrying and wanting what they think is best for someone." Studying him, she ran the tip of her tongue along her lips. "Did it cheer you up? The kiss," she specified.

No two ways about it, Tony had no idea how to handle this woman. Or what to expect next. "You're not supposed to ask questions like that."

Her eyes were innocent. "Why not?"

He needed something to do with his hands other than hold her again, so he began rummaging through the stacked plastic storage drawers. Knowing he wouldn't have been able to focus in on the hooks unless they stuck him in the thumb.

"Because questions like that are too blunt."

"They're to the point," she corrected. "Because I'd like to know."

He wasn't accustomed to that kind of directness. It caught him off guard. "Why?"

"It would be nice to know if you were as affected by it as I was." She smiled at the stunned expression on his face. "Something else I'm not supposed to admit to, right?" Mimicking him, she began opening various drawers and looking through them. All she found were more decorations. "Sorry, I was too busy raising my brothers and sisters and trying to get grades good enough for a scholarship, to learn the fine art of male-female relationships."

"Is that why you come on like gangbusters?"

It was her turn to stop and stare at him. She wrapped her tongue around the word he'd used. "Gangbusters. Haven't heard that one since the last time I watched a Jimmy Cagney movie."

"You watch Jimmy Cagney movies?" He scrutinized her face to see if she was putting him on. One of his cousins might have mentioned something to her.

"Doesn't everyone?"

Her expression was inscrutable. Why didn't that surprise him? He went back to rummaging, this time actually focusing on the contents of the drawers. "No."

"Well, I do." Kneeling, she began working her way through the bottom drawers. "Apparently you do, too, or you wouldn't have used the term as if you expected me to know what it meant." She glanced up and saw that the suspicion had deepened in his eyes. "I watch detective movies, too."

"And science fiction."

She nodded. "And science fiction."

"I hate to say it, but we seem to have some things in common." Yet they were as different as night and day, he thought.

Shutting the bottom drawer, she began to rise to her feet. He took her hand and helped her up. Chivalry was making a silent comeback, she thought.

"Why do you hate to say it, Tony? Because you don't want to get close to anyone? You're close to your family."

That had been a given from the very beginning. "Not the same thing."

"No, I don't suppose it is." But it meant he had feelings, and that they could rise to the surface. It was a hopeful sign. Glancing past his shoulder, she saw the elusive box of hooks. Reaching around him, Mikky closed her hand around the so-called missing box. "Found them."

Pivoting on her heel, Mikky began to leave. Maybe she was crowding him. Maybe she was wrong in thinking she could bring him around for his own sake and for hers. If the horse didn't want to drink, you couldn't drown him in the trough.

He caught her wrist just before she started going up the stairs.

Blowing out a breath, she half turned to look at him. At this height, she was just a shade taller than he was and had to look down. "What?"

"If I could, it would be you."

The remark undid everything she'd just been trying to put into place. Maybe she wasn't so wrong in her thinking at that.

Mikky smiled down at him then. It was a soft smile rather than a brash, cocky one, and it managed to pry open a little farther the crack that was already steadily widening. "I'll keep that in mind."

He could feel his temper fraying already, and they'd only been through the ordeal of trying to find a parking space. Why the hell had he let her talk him into this? Because he was growing soft in the head, that's why. There must have been something in his aunt's dinner last Sunday, something he ate that was in turn eating away his common sense.

There was no other explanation why he'd allowed himself to be roped into this on a Saturday morning.

"I don't have time for this," he growled at Mikky. There had to be more people jammed into this mall than there were in the entire state of Maryland.

"As I said earlier, you'll just have to make time." She faced him squarely, not an easy feat with Justin in a carryall between them. "Christmas is less than a week away, and you don't have a present to your name."

It still amazed him that, though he had every intention of standing firm against her, somehow he'd found himself driving over here. "None of my family is expecting anything from me."

It was a lousy excuse, and Mikky wasn't even about to dignify its existence by discussing it. The man was going to take part in Christmas if it killed her. She wasn't certain just when she had appointed herself his secret guardian angel, but she had, and getting him to take part in Christmas was now not just a goal but a mission.

"All the more reason to do it. It'll be a surprise." She was trying very hard not to be judgmental. She had never approved of sitting on the sidelines and letting life move on without you. "Don't you at least want to give your Aunt Bridgette something for Christmas?"

"Well, maybe," he finally said before rallying again. "But I haven't the slightest idea what to get for her. Or any of them."

Triumph entered her eyes. She'd finally gotten him to admit at least that much. "That's why you're bringing me along."

Tony looked at Mikky incredulously. The woman had appeared on his doorstep and all but thrown a net over him, dragging him to his car like a bagged possum with absolutely no control over his fate. "Who's bringing whom?"

With a careless wave of her hand, she dismissed his question. "Let's not start quibbling over fine points. The main thing is that we're both here."

And whose fault was that, Tony thought.

Mikky began to lead the way to the first store on her mental list. Having no choice, Tony fell into place beside her. He looked at Justin, who was curled against her chest in the carryall. It crossed his mind that of the two of them, Justin and himself, Justin had the better arrangement. "I can carry him, you know."

She placed her hand over the baby's back. "Yes, I know, but he's fine right here. When he gets too much for me, I'll let you take over."

That's what she said, but that's not what she meant. Heaven help him, but Tony was beginning to know how she operated. "You wouldn't admit it even if something did get to be too much for you. You feel called upon to do it all."

Had he said that to her three weeks ago, Mikky would have taken offense at the criticism. But she'd mellowed a little and gotten to know him, as well. He used criticism like some people used sunblock. To protect himself from getting burned.

Mikky inclined her head toward him. "I'll let you in on a little secret, I'm not as independent as I want everyone to believe I am."

Tony didn't buy into that for a minute. He'd watched her at the site, and while she might look like every man's idea of a delectable cream puff, she took pride in being able to shoulder her own responsibilities. Took pride, too, in the fact that she was a hell of a lot stronger than she looked. "You'd bite off the first hand that was stretched out to help you."

"Maybe not." Pausing, she looked at him, really looked at him, and saw things that her initial sparring matches with him had made her miss. Like the fact that he had a sensitive soul under all that barbwire. "Maybe I'd take it. If it was the right hand." She grinned. "Even superheroes have an off day."

Banishing the serious moment, Mikky looked around. She stopped walking and turned to get his input. "So, where do you want to go first?"

"Home."

She laughed. The man never gave up. "Okay, where do you want to go second?"

Tony couldn't remember the last time he'd been to a mall. Even when he was married, shopping was strictly his wife's domain. Simple in his tastes, he hadn't bought new clothes of any kind in over a year.

Even standing still, he was being jostled. "This is really a bad idea."

One hand against Justin's back, Mikky threaded her other arm through his. "It's a really good idea, once you get the hang of it." Very subtly she began to steer him off toward Cairo's Department Store located in the southernmost part of the mall.

Tony couldn't get over how many people there were, all rushing, struggling, looking exhausted. "Why do people do this?"

"Because it's fun."

He looked at Mikky as if she was crazy. "How can you tell?"

"It's a gift." Laughing at the face he made, she dragged him off to the department store.

Amazed that she'd actually managed to find a table for them to sit at, Tony lowered himself into the chair opposite hers. He shed the shopping bags that hung from his wrists like overweight paper bracelets on either side of his chair and barely had enough energy to raise the coffee cup to his lips. He could stand on his feet for sixteen hours straight on a site, but following Mikky around a mall for a few hours was a completely different matter. Every part of him was drained to the max.

She, on the other hand, looked as if she could go another round or two equal to what they had just endured. How? She'd plowed her way from counter to counter like a heat-seeking missile on a mission. "I think you bring new meaning to the word *pushy*."

"Forceful, assertive," she corrected, supplying adjectives for him. Taking Justin out of the carrier, she made him comfortable on her lap.

"Pushy," he insisted.

She rummaged through the large bag Tony had brought with him until she found a bottle of juice for Justin. "But we got gifts for everyone, and we did it in under three hours. That's pretty good, considering how close to Christmas it is."

Tony felt a little overwhelmed by all the festive decorations in the mall. Maybe because it made him remember. He looked at her thoughtfully as he held his cup between two hands.

"You like this season, don't you?"

Mikky almost said, *What wasn't there to like*, but caught herself. "It's my favorite time of year." She debated letting it go, but decided that she couldn't. "I take it you have reservations."

It was none of her business, and Tony had no idea why he was telling her this. Maybe it was to shut her up, maybe it was because the feelings had been trapped too long inside of him.

"The accident happened just before last Thanksgiving. I spent last Christmas at the cemetery."

She surprised him by reaching over and putting her hand on his in silent comfort. He didn't take her hand, but he didn't pull his away, either. "I don't think Teri would have wanted you to spend the rest of your life in the cemetery."

He knew what she was saying. "No, she wouldn't have. She had a good heart. She..." His voice trailed away and he looked at Mikky. "You're nothing like her." Frustrated at his own inarticulation, he shook his head. "That didn't come out right. Teri was quiet, almost shy. She didn't have an 'assertive'—" he chose one of Mikky's words "—bone in her body. And yet..."

He left the word hanging. "Yet?"

Tony shook his head. He'd said too much already. Done too much. Allowed her to get too far into his life. Look at how far she'd burrowed in such a short time. He couldn't allow that to continue.

He drained the cup and put it down before continuing. "Never mind, must be the lack of air."

He was going to say something to her, something nice, and they both knew that lack of air had nothing to do with it. Mikky felt a little cheated and a little gratified at the same time. At least she'd gotten him this far.

"Drop in blood sugar," she suggested. "Temporary insanity. Allergic reaction to paper shopping bags...."

He began to laugh, partially surrendering, at least for the moment. "You really are something else, aren't you?"

"That's what I've been trying to tell you. I'm something else." Mikky looked at him significantly. "Not better, not worse, just something else." It was up to him to realize just what that actually meant to him. For the time being, she would glory in her success at getting him to go Christmas shopping.

Not to be outdone by the adults, Justin had drained his bottle. Mikky returned it to the bag. She was ready to go. "Okay, gents, let's get this show on the road."

Tony looked at her hopefully, suddenly feeling energized. "We're finished?"

She tried not to laugh at his expression. "We're finished."

But he was wary that she might try to trick him into complacency and then drag him off to yet another store. "We can go home?"

Leaning over, she patted his cheek. "Yes, Toto, we can go home." She rose to her feet, afraid that if she lingered over Tony, she might do something stupid like lean over and kiss him. A woman had to leave some moves to a man, or else they didn't count.

Tony had never felt so relieved at leaving a parking lot in his life. Glancing in the rearview mirror, he watched the mall fade into the background, like a bad dream that should have never been.

And then he thought of all the things in his trunk. He slanted a glance toward Mikky. "I don't suppose you like wrapping things."

"Things," she repeated, stretching the moment. "As in presents?"

His hands tightened on the wheel. She was going to make him spell this out, too, wasn't she? "Yeah."

"Yes, I like wrapping." Like every part of the holiday, wrapping presents gave her pleasure. She doubted if there was a thing about Christmas she didn't like, except taking down the decorations after the holiday was over.

"Good, then would you—"

"No."

Easing down on the brake at the light, he looked at her. "No?"

"No, I won't wrap them for you." The car behind them beeped its horn. The light had turned green again. Tony muttered something under his breath about the lack of patience in the world. Mikky thought it rather ironic, coming from him. "But I'll help you wrap."

"And the difference being?"

She glanced behind her to make sure Justin was still sleeping in his seat. The boy was out like a light. "That I won't let you foist the job onto me. I'll assist, supervise—"

"Straw bossing. Your favorite pastime."

Mikky's smile got to him. Tony found that happening a lot, lately, and wished he could find a way to prevent it. "You *are* getting to know me, aren't you?"

Yeah, he was. Against his will. He said nothing, not wanting to build on the thought her words suggested. He reminded himself that even if he did, there was no harm in it. This was just a temporary situation, and he knew it. They both did. By her own admission, Mikky was moving on. That meant right after Christmas there would be no more threat, no more source of irritation to him.

No one to stir his blood or make him wonder...

He couldn't have it both ways. He was either happy she was leaving or he wasn't. The impromptu self-imposed lecture bore no fruit. He couldn't decide.

Couldn't admit—

Tony took her to his house so she could pick up her car, then followed her back to her house. Strictly to have her give him pointers on wrapping the gifts.

Although he saw it as even more a waste of time than shopping had been.

"Don't see why it matters who wraps it. I paid for it." He set Justin, car seat and all, down on the floor. The boy was sound asleep.

"Spoken like a true Scrooge." She led Tony over to

the kitchen table and cleared away the place mats. "Don't you want to feel the true spirit of Christmas?"

"I figure that'll happen once the credit card statements start coming in."

Mikky shook her head. "I refuse to believe you're as cynical, as hopeless, as you try to pretend."

"I'm not pretending."

Apparently she knew better than he did, Mikky thought. She stopped setting up and looked him straight in the eye. "If you weren't pretending, my friend, that baby over there would have spent his first night with social services three weeks ago."

Justin was another matter. Tony was still waiting for his mother to come. And hoping that she wouldn't. What harm would it do if he retained custody of the boy? If he was there for him when he needed someone?

"There're exceptions to every rule."

"You're trying too hard."

"Apparently—" he looked at her pointedly "—not hard enough."

She faced him squarely. "You couldn't scare me away the first day, Marino, and I'm not running for cover now. There's a warm, tender man in there. All he needs is to figure out how to find his way toward the light again."

He raised his brows. "You being the light?"

The grin took over most of her, starting at her toes. "No, but that's a nice thought, thank you."

He scowled. Why couldn't she just back off? Why did she have to keep picking at him and picking at him, until he didn't know which end was up? "I wasn't trying to give you a compliment."

"Too late," she said cheerfully. "I take what I can."

He tried to give her a dark look and succeeded only marginally. "I noticed."

"Good. Now let's get down to business, shall we?" He looked at her blankly. She held up one of the rolls of wrapping paper they'd bought. "Wrapping. Otherwise, Christmas will be over, and you'll still be staring at these naked boxes."

"God forbid I should give naked boxes." Tony didn't see what the fuss was about, anyway. It was the gift inside that ultimately counted. Newspaper wrapping on the outside would do equally as well. "This is just a conspiracy by the greeting card companies to get people to spend money, you know that, don't you?"

"And maybe Christmas is just a conspiracy by God to get people to be just a little friendlier for a few days out of the year," she countered. "Concentrate on that for a while, okay?"

Grudgingly he muttered, "Okay."

He was coming along, Mikky thought. She had the presence of mind to hide her smile as she went to get the transparent tape and scissors. She left him muttering something to himself. Mikky knew better than to ask him to speak up.

Chapter Eleven

The security guard waved to her as Mikky drove past his station and onto the lot. Absently she noticed that the old man had taken to staying on the lot longer these last few weeks. Certainly past the time when he was legally obligated to remain.

As everyone else did, he liked Justin, often coming by to play with him. She supposed there was not much for a man like Pete Reynolds to do. In one of the conversations they'd had, he'd told her he was retired and lived alone. Being a guard gave him a purpose and helped him make ends meet.

Obviously lonely, Pete liked to talk, and Mikky didn't mind listening. But this morning she didn't feel very sociable. Not with what was on her mind. Thad had called her last night, right after she'd come home from another dinner at Bridgette's. The sense of contentment she'd had from spending the day with Tony's family had dissipated quickly after her brother had told her why he was calling. Though she hated what he had to tell her, she knew it hadn't been easy for him. Because she'd brought him into it, Thad had no choice.

Tony was right. She should have kept her mouth shut. But she'd done it for the best of reasons, and now there was no real way to undo this, even though she wanted to. What was done was done.

"Mik, I'm going to have to report this," Thad had told her glumly after asking if she had come up with anything on her end. For his part, there had been no information, no reports, no leads. "It's been three weeks since that baby was abandoned and nobody's come forward. He has to be put into the system."

There was a long pause on the other end. "I can pretend to keep my eyes closed to this until after Christmas, but then, that's it. If this isn't resolved..."

He didn't have to finish his sentence. She knew. Mikky had sighed, regret gnawing at her. "I'm sorry I told you about the baby, Thad."

"Off the record, yeah, me too."

Mikky hadn't slept last night. She'd spent it tossing and turning, searching for the right words to tell Tony that the fragile life he was enjoying was going to be over soon. The coward's way would have been to keep quiet, to allow him to enjoy Christmas, basking in ignorance. But then reality would be too sharp, too sudden. Too cruel. She wanted him to be prepared.

Though he was probably going to kill the messenger, that didn't change the fact that it was cruelly deceptive not to tell Tony that he only had until the day after Christmas.

She didn't want secrets between them.

There wasn't going to be anything between them once Justin was gone. At least, not on Tony's part. He was going to blame her for this latest loss in his life. And he'd be right.

Damn it, when was she going to learn not to interfere?

Parking the car, Mikky sighed and sat there for a moment. Everything within her felt as if a lead coating had been poured over it.

She felt like crying. Crying for Tony, for Justin and maybe for herself.

But tears weren't going to do anything. A miracle or two was needed, not tears. As far as she knew, the world was fresh out of miracles.

"You okay, Ms. R?"

Startled, she realized that the guard had come up to her. Even his dog, so fierce looking when she'd driven onto the lot, was now looking into the car, his paws on the door, his hot breath fogging up the top of her window where she had it cracked open. The dog was making a low, soft noise that sounded oddly sympathetic.

Funny how animals could sense when things were wrong, she thought. Too bad people didn't come equipped with the same gift.

She shook her head in answer to the guard's question. "No, not really."

Pete backed up, tugging on Max's leash as Mikky opened her door. "Lot of that flu going round. Maybe you shouldn't be around the baby when he comes."

She smiled sadly. Justin was the highlight of everyone's day. Why couldn't there be a way out of this? There had to be something she could do....

She reminded herself that it was her doing that had gotten them to this impasse in the first place. "The baby's why I feel this way."

Concern etched itself onto the moonlike face. He

peered at her as he walked with her to her trailer. Max strained at his leash. "Something wrong with the baby?"

"No, but…" Mikky hesitated. Maybe if she practiced telling Pete, she could tell Tony. She turned to face him. "My brother's a police detective, and he knows about Justin. He told me last night that if the baby's mother doesn't come forward soon, he's going to have to take Justin right after Christmas."

Pete took the news harder than she'd anticipated. "Take him? Take him where?"

He sounded almost defensive, Mikky thought. A preview of what was to come once she told Tony. "Social services. They'll find foster parents for him."

"But he's got Mr. Marino. And you." By his bewildered tone, it was obvious that Pete didn't understand why any of this had to happen. In her heart neither did Mikky.

This was going to be harder than she thought. A lot harder. If she couldn't make the harsh reality of the situation acceptable to the guard, how was she ever going to make Tony understand—and not hate her? "He needs parents."

That still didn't answer anything for Pete. "Maybe you or Mr. Marino could adopt him. Or both of you." With each word, his voice went up, building in intensity. Max began to prance, obviously anticipating that something was about to happen.

Mikky knew Pete was only worried about Justin. They all were. "It's not that simple. As long as Justin's parents are out there somewhere…" Mikky paused, doubting if the guard could understand all the ramifications that came into play. Or think them fair. Not that she blamed him. They weren't fair, not in this instance.

So much for a dry run, she thought, giving up. "Well, it's not that simple, that's all."

"What if..." Pete looked at her, stumbling over the words in his mouth. "What if his mother was dead, and nobody knew who the father was?"

Mikky shrugged. "Well, I suppose..." Something in his voice caught her attention. She looked at him, scrutinizing the expression on his face. "Pete, what do you know about Justin?"

He took a step back nervously, shaking his head. Max yelped as Pete narrowly missed the dog's paw. "Nothing, I—"

Mikky caught him by his arm. He knew something, something he wasn't telling. Suddenly hopeful, she tried to get the man to talk. "Pete, this is important. Did you see who dropped Justin off at Mr. Marino's trailer that night?"

"No." And then, making his decision, Pete straightened and squared his shoulders. "But I know who did."

All this time and he'd known all along. "Who?" she demanded, stunned by the confession.

Pete hesitated for a moment longer and then blurted out, "I did."

Tony's cheeks felt as if they were tingling as he hurried from the car to his trailer. Normally the cold weather invigorated him. It was one of the things he liked best about living in Colorado. The winters were picturesque. But now the cold weather was a source of concern for him. He worried that it was too cold for the boy he had pressed against his chest.

Making it into the trailer, Tony sighed with relief as he closed the door behind him. This was the last day he'd have to come to the site until after the holidays. It was a relief to look forward to Christmas instead of anticipating it with dread.

Justin had done that for him. Justin and Mikky.

Tony was walking a tightrope, and he knew it. But for the time being he was determined to pretend that he was on solid ground.

Tony set the seat he'd brought in with him on the floor and rested Justin's well-padded behind on his desk. "Let's get you out of that, partner."

Justin gurgled his agreement. Very carefully Tony took off the heavy jacket Mikky had bought for the baby during the infamous shopping venture on Saturday. Remembering the grueling hours he'd followed her around brought a curve to his mouth before he dismissed the memory.

Just as he tossed the jacket onto his chair, the door to his trailer flew open without the usual knock. A gust of cold air came in with it. It seemed appropriate, he thought. She reminded him of a barely contained northern twister.

"Make yourself at home, Mikky," he told her before he turned around.

"Tony, we have to talk."

Unable to read her tone, he still didn't like the sound of that. Holding Justin in his arms, he turned around and saw that she wasn't alone.

Why was she in here with the watchman?

Tony looked from the man to Mikky, not sure what to make of the situation. Had someone been stealing supplies? "What's up?"

Pete swept his hat from his head. He was bald, except for a fringe of gray hair. He was also exceedingly uncomfortable, Tony noted. He waited, not knowing exactly what it was that he was waiting for. Stalling, Pete chucked Justin under the chin. The baby's eyes lit as he cooed and grabbed Pete's finger.

"Do you want to hold Justin?" Maybe that would make the guard feel more at ease, Tony thought.

But Pete shook his head. The words came fast, like a flash flood, engulfing its audience. "His name isn't Justin, it's Pete. Like mine. I thought maybe if you thought he had the same name as your son, you'd take to him faster."

Stunned, Tony wasn't sure he was following what the man was trying to tell him. Or that he wanted to. "What do you mean, take to him faster?"

"Justin is Pete's grandson," Mikky interjected.

Tony's brows narrowed as he fixed his gaze on the old man. "Explain."

Clearly upset, Pete began. "Lita was such a good girl when she was young, but she was always trying too hard, trying to get people to like her—"

Tony looked at Mikky for a translation. "Lita was his daughter," she told him.

Tony's arm tightened around the baby he held, his mind embracing the single word that made any sense in the disjointed narrative. *Was.*

Haplessly, the guard forged ahead. "She got in with the wrong crowd, did some things..." Because it was too hurtful to recount, Pete let his voice trail off. "When she found out she was pregnant, she tried very hard to stay clean. And she did," Pete told them enthusiastically. He'd been so proud of Lita, so hopeful. With a sad smile, he touched Justin's downy head. "He didn't have any addictions or anything when he was born. I really thought he'd be a turnaround for her." As he spoke, Pete's face seemed to fall. "But she was never very strong, and she started hanging out with the same people again. Doing the same things again.''

His throat choked with emotion, Pete stared down at his shoes. "I found her when I came home one morning. She'd taken too much and um…'' When he looked up at Tony, there were tears in his eyes. He couldn't say the words, couldn't tell them that when he'd come home to his daughter, she'd already been dead several hours. Lita was beyond pain now. He had to try and remember that. "I love that boy, but I'm too old to do this on my own. There is nobody else now." He looked at Mikky, silently appealing to her for help. "I'd heard that Mr. Marino had lost his own boy. I thought that maybe, you know, they could help each other.''

"So you abandoned him here?" Tony accused him incredulously.

"Oh, no, sir, I wasn't abandoning Pete. I was just trying to make things right for everyone. Him. You.'' Frightened, bewildered and contrite all at the same time, the guard chewed on his lower lip. He twisted his cap completely out of shape. "I'm sorry.''

Moved, only able to guess at what the man had had to go through, Mikky slipped her arm around the guard's shoulders. "It's okay.''

But it was to Tony that Pete directed his question and fears. "What happens now? Am I going to go to jail?''

"No," Mikky said firmly. "Not if my brother wants to live out the week." The smile on her lips was meant to encourage the old man. "Now that you've come forward and told your story, Thad doesn't have to file that report.'' The full impact of her words dawned on her and she looked at Tony. Tony wasn't going to have to give Justin up. She hadn't ruined everything for him. "There are mitigating circumstances.'' She looked at

the guard. "Have you changed your mind about Jus—
Pete? Do you want him back?"

Warmth and affection filled his eyes as he looked
at his grandson. "With all my heart—but nothing's
changed." He shook his head. "I'm too old. The doctor
says my heart's pretty bad." He shrugged philosophically. He'd lived a long life. Leaving his grandson alone
had been his only concern. "There's no telling how
much time I have left. I want Justin—" he looked at
her significantly, using the boy's new name "—to have
a good home. I still think it would be, with Mr. Marino."

If he'd had any doubts about the future, they were
gone now. Listening to Pete, Tony had made up his
mind, "I'll take good care of him, Pete. And you can
come to see him as often as you'd like."

"I'd like that very much." He drew closer to the boy.
"Hear that, Justin? You're going to have a good home.
Better than I could ever give you." He raised his eyes
to Tony. "I don't have much, but it's yours."

Tony shook his head. "You've already given me the
most precious thing you have, Pete. I'm the one in your
debt, not the other way around."

If Mikky had ever doubted that Tony had a heart, she
had her proof now. She hated the fact that she had to
be the devil's advocate in this. "Justin's still going to
have to go through the system—"

Tony frowned. The system meant complications. And
that meant he could still lose Justin. "How about a private adoption?"

She'd done some research on the subject. "You're a
single man."

"Widower," Tony corrected. It was the first time

since the accident he'd ever used the word. The pain he expected wasn't quite as harsh.

Tony looked at her as if she were the one who was trying to take Justin away from him instead of just the opposite. "Still, that might not make a difference."

He knew she meant well, but he couldn't help the note of annoyance that came into his voice. "Since when did you become the voice of reason?"

"Since one of us has to be." Did he think she enjoyed this? She just wanted to make sure that nothing occurred to trip him up. "You can't just float along with your eyes shut."

Right about now, it sounded like a plan to him. But she was right, and he knew it. "I'll talk to Dottie. She once told me she has some connections in social services."

Pete's hat was almost unwearable by this point. "Then it's going to be all right?" he asked them eagerly.

Mikky nodded. "It's going to be all right." Mentally she crossed her fingers. At least, it would turn out all right for Tony and Justin.

She told herself that was all that mattered.

Sitting in her living room, Dottie listened patiently as she tried to glean what her cousin and Mikky were saying to her in what seemed to be two very different frequencies. Both Mikky and Tony seemed determined to be the first to explain the situation to her.

She was getting a headache. Dottie held up her hand, stopping the flood of words. "Okay, so we know the baby's parents—"

"Mother," Mikky corrected. "According to Pete,

Lita never knew who the father was, and nobody ever stepped forward.''

"Pete?" Dottie repeated.

"Reynolds," Tony supplied before Mikky could. Justin was playing on the floor between them, oblivious to the discussion going on around him that would play such a large hand in his fate.

Dottie looked from Tony to Mikky, trying to see if she had this right. "So this Pete Reynolds is now the baby's legal guardian.''

Mikky drew Justin away from Tony's shoe before he could start chewing. He was beginning to teethe again, she thought. She knew the signs. "He has the papers," she told Dottie.

Dottie looked at Tony as he picked Justin up and placed him on his lap. "And he's giving custody up to you.''

"Right." And he meant to do whatever he had to in order to keep that custody.

Dottie had the pieces she needed for now. As a child psychologist, she was sometimes called in by social services to help evaluate family situations and the people who were involved in them. There were a few key people in the department she could turn to in this matter.

"Shouldn't be a problem." She smiled, watching Tony. The little boy had brought about a drastic change in her cousin. She had no doubts that the woman sitting next to him had had a hand in the alterations as well, but if she knew Tony, it was going to take a major act of Congress to get him to admit it. "You've got a good, solid background. But they'll still have to look into it.''

Tony shrugged. He didn't see that as a problem. "I've got no skeletons.''

"You also don't have a wife," Dottie pointed out.

"Things aren't as strict as they once were, but it would still go smoother if you were married."

But he wasn't. Not anymore. "What about the grandfather's wishes?" he reminded her.

"They definitely help, but they don't cinch it." She saw her cousin's face cloud over. It wasn't hopeless, just tricky. "Let me see what I can do." She came to the part she knew he didn't want to hear. "In the meantime, I can tell you that they're going to want to place Justin with another family until this is all decided."

That didn't make any sense to him. "Why can't he stay with me?"

"Rules, Tony." Valiantly ignoring the upsurge in her stomach, Dottie leaned over and placed a comforting hand over his. "I'll see if I can get them to place Justin with Shea and me." She was pretty certain she could. "I'll need the practice changing diapers."

Tony thought it looked as if there was light at the end of the tunnel, and for once it wasn't from an oncoming train rushing at him.

"So, I guess that's that," Mikky murmured as they walked away from Dottie and Shea's house.

She'd insisted on coming with him for this last part of his odyssey. They had brought Justin over and left him behind with the social worker who had come to advise Dottie and Shea on their responsibilities. True to her word, Dottie had pulled every string within her reach and gotten Justin placed with her. Papers were being pushed through, and it appeared as if Justin could stop playing musical houses soon and be with Tony for good.

But for now, following the letter of the court order, the little boy had to remain with Dottie and her husband.

As he walked to his car, Tony's arms felt strangely empty. Funny how accustomed he'd gotten to the weight he'd been carrying around for such a short time. He knew he'd be seeing the boy again soon, but even a short separation was difficult to bear.

Mikky unlocked her door. They had driven in separate cars. Running late, she'd come straight from an impromptu meeting with a new developer, refusing to allow Tony to face this step alone.

Alone. As if her presence mattered, she mocked herself. He had his family to turn to. She was what she'd always been to him, an intrusive outsider. With the question of Justin's future all but resolved, there was no further need of her.

Tony had no further need of her. The thought repeated in her brain.

And what of her? What of her needs? Didn't matter, she told herself. She'd known that at the outset. If she'd fallen in love with a man who had no place in his heart for her, that was her problem, nobody else's.

She bit back a sigh. "So, I'll see you around," she said.

He'd been prepared to ask her to come over. He wasn't sure what he was doing, only that he wanted to venture forward a little further. Explore these feelings inside him a little more. Her almost-flippant remark made him reexamine the wisdom of asking her to stay the night.

If she could back away so easily, so glibly, that meant she obviously didn't have the same feelings he had. He'd almost made a colossal mistake—as well as a fool of himself.

Faced with that, Tony retreated. "Yeah, maybe we'll run into each other on another project."

And then again, maybe not. The thought hurt Mikky. "I'll remember to sharpen my protractor," she murmured.

He didn't hear her. "What?"

But she shook her head. "Never mind, poor joke. Tell your aunt Merry Christmas for me." Mikky slid into the car.

Tony thought of asking her not to leave and told himself he was an idiot. She apparently couldn't wait to get away.

"Yeah, sure."

But she was already gone.

Chapter Twelve

What the hell was he doing?

Annoyed, Tony stopped shaving the five-o'clock shadow from his face and turned off the tap water. He took a good, long look at himself in the mirror. Sighing, he leaned both hands against the sides of the sink.

He was running, that was what he was doing. Running from something that had no substance, no form. Running like a coward. He stared into his eyes, searching for answers that he was keeping from himself.

No, he amended, maybe it did have substance. An entire mountain of substance. He was running from love.

Running from love because he was afraid of doing without it. That made no sense. Wasn't he doing without it right now? And how did it feel? he mocked himself.

Like he'd suddenly found himself sinking into the fiery pits of hell, that's how it felt. Deep and burning and bare.

Tony scrubbed his hands over his face. Justin was almost his. He'd thought...he'd thought that having the boy in his life would be enough. Adopting Justin meant he was getting a second chance to be a father. A chance to heal for a reason, instead of just gravitating toward numbness.

But Justin, wonderful though the little boy was, wasn't enough.

He wanted more.

He knew what love was all about, knew what loving was all about, and he wanted more.

And he was going to get it.

Still wearing only the towel he'd draped over himself when he came out of the shower, Tony walked into his bedroom and marched over to the telephone on the nightstand. He hit the number that dialed his aunt automatically. Tony spoke as soon as he heard her say hello.

"Aunt Bridgette, I'm going to be late."

There were no words of admonishment, no mention that this was Christmas Eve and he shouldn't keep them waiting. Instead he heard her laugh.

"It's about time, Tony."

The house was filled with music. Nonstop music. At last count Mikky owned thirty Christmas CDs. She was playing all of them, one after another, thanks to the multistorage CD player she had in her living room. *It's A Wonderful Life* was playing on both of her television sets. Happiness, good will and cheer resounded on the airwaves, wedging itself into every nook and every corner.

She was trying to block out the hurt.

It didn't help.

Her insides still felt like the floor of a warehouse after an out-of-control fire had been set by an arsonist. There was nothing left but ashes.

She was easy, no doubt about it. Selling out her heart so easily to a man whose only use for it was to make it into a coaster.

Her own fault, she admonished herself. All her own fault. Nobody asked her to fall for the big jerk. Least of all him. But she'd fallen, anyway. Hard, fast and completely.

She sat on the floor, staring up at the Christmas tree she'd put up several days ago, the lights glistening because she was looking at them through the tears in her eyes. She knew she was feeling sorry for herself, but she couldn't help it. Christmas somehow found her very vulnerable this year.

You didn't get to choose who you loved, she thought, hugging her knees. But you could choose who you made yourself a fool in front of, and she'd at least stopped short of that at the last minute. It wasn't much of a consolation, but at least it was something. After they'd left Justin at his cousin's house, she'd almost given in to temptation and asked Tony to come over here.

At least she'd saved herself the embarrassment of having him turn her down.

Or worse, take her up on it, make love to her and then tip his hat in the morning, leaving as if nothing had happened.

Because for him, nothing had.

If it had, if he'd felt for her what she was feeling right now, he would have called her. Would have tried to see her.

Mikky rested her head against her knees. Three days

and not a word from him. The site was shut down because the rainy season had decided to hit with a vengeance. But the construction crew was far ahead of schedule, so the rain was a welcome respite to everyone.

Everyone but her. She'd been hoping for an excuse to see Tony one more time before she left for Reno. The developer funding her next project wanted her on the site right after New Year's. Asking if she was free, he had even invited her to be a guest at his vacation home over the holidays.

Well, she was free all right. Christmas Day, she'd visit with her family, hand out gifts to all her brothers and sisters and their families, and then, she was free.

Free, damn it.

Rubbing away a stray tear with the heel of her hand, Mikky got up. Enough was enough. She'd wallowed and indulged herself and now it was time to act like an adult instead of some maudlin heroine in a silent movie.

"So, you've been hurt. Big deal. Get over it," she ordered, gritting her teeth together.

Mikky straightened her shoulders. Taking in a deep lungful of air, she began to sing along with the Christmas medley that was currently playing. She got half the words wrong.

She didn't hear the doorbell when it rang. It registered belatedly as a sound on the peripheral edges of Bing Crosby's rendition of "White Christmas," melded with the song and the banging she heard on her door.

Now what?

She crossed to the door, forcing herself to feel sociable. With effort, she pasted a smile on her face. She wasn't expecting anyone. She'd made the rounds, though it had been hard for her, bringing her usual plates of baked goods to her neighbors and collecting their offerings in return. The plates, all gaily wrapped, were stacked up on her coffee table, untouched. She didn't much feel like eating tonight.

Maybe it was the carolers. Some of the neighborhood kids liked to go from door to door, singing. Heaven knew she had plenty of food to give them in exchange for an off-key rendition of "Silent Night."

Mentally psyching herself up, Mikky flipped the lock and pulled open the door. "I didn't think you were coming around." And then her mouth dropped open.

"You were expecting me?" That put her one up on him, Tony thought. He hadn't known he was coming until half an hour ago.

It took her a second to realize that she wasn't just imagining him there. He was real.

She still stood staring at him. "No, um...I thought it was the Christmas carolers."

The last thing he would have said she was waiting for was carolers. "You need more music?" Still standing on her doorstep, he peered in. "Sounds as if you've got the Mormon Tabernacle Choir in here already."

Mikky flushed. She reached over to the control panel beside the door and turned everything off. As an afterthought, she stepped back to let him in.

The house was filled with silence. And the beating of her heart. She regretted not having turned up the television set louder. What was he doing here? She could only think of one thing. "Is something wrong with Justin?"

"No." He shook his head. "I just decided you could tell her yourself."

He'd completely lost her. "Tell who what?"

"Aunt Bridgette. I decided you could tell her Merry Christmas yourself. It's the last thing you said to me before you left." He turned to look at her squarely, praying he wasn't making a fool of himself. That he hadn't misread everything that had been developing on the sidelines while he'd been busy denying it. Praying that she wanted him as much as he wanted her. "Damn it, woman, work with me here."

No, she wasn't going to be an idiot. She wasn't going to put words into his mouth. Or think he was saying something he wasn't. She was through taking death-defying leaps to conclusions that weren't. "I would, if I knew what you were saying."

"What am I, talking a foreign language here?"

Mikky pressed her lips together. *Tell me, Tony. Make me understand. Tell me you want me. I can't come to you if you don't tell me.* "Right now, yes. At least another dialect I'm not familiar with."

He took her hand, afraid that she might vanish for one reason or another if he didn't hold on to her. "I want you to come over and spend Christmas Eve at Aunt Bridgette's house."

"All right," Mikky said slowly. Was that it, or was there more? *Oh please God, let there be more.* "Let me just get my coat—"

As she passed him to go to the closet, he pulled her around and into his arms. She looked at him, bewildered, a silent question in her eyes.

"If I don't say this quickly," he told her, hating the fact that he was fumbling inside, "I'm going to lose my nerve."

"Then say it quickly." Mikky barely breathed out the words.

But it didn't come out quickly. It came out slowly, haltingly, just the way his love had unfurled. "I got the feeling...these last few weeks, I kind of got the feeling..."

She began to feel her heart accelerating. "Yes? What kind of feeling?"

"That we were a unit. You, Justin and me. That we formed a family." Why wasn't this coming out right? Frustrated with his own inability to articulate his feelings, he bit off a curse. "Damn it, Mikky, you're not making it easy for me."

The look in her eyes was innocent. But her mouth was beginning to curve. "What? What am I doing?"

"You're looking at me in that way of yours."

"What way?"

He combed his fingers through her hair, moving a strand away from her face. Caressing her "The way that makes me forget my name. The way that makes my knees weak and makes me want to crush you against me."

Thank you, God. Her smile widened. "I could shut my eyes."

He shook his head, gathering her closer in his arms. It was going to be all right, he thought. Finally all right. "That's worse. Then I'd be tempted to kiss you, and I wouldn't get any of it out."

Mikky started to relax, even though her heart was hammering faster than a riveter's drill. She threaded her arms around his neck, leaning into him.

"Then by all means, get it out so we can get it over with. You haven't kissed me in five days, seven hours and twenty-seven minutes."

So she'd been as aware of the time they'd wasted as he was. "Five days, seven hours—"

She pretended to glance at her wristwatch. "And twenty-eight minutes now."

As difficult as she'd made it before, she made it easier now. A lot easier. "Mikky, I never thought that I could feel anything again, but you found a way to prove me wrong."

She grinned, catching her lower lip between her teeth. "You're wrong a lot."

"No, I'm not," he contradicted. "And certainly not about this. I'm in love with you, Mikky. I don't know when, I don't know how, but it happened. One minute I wasn't, the next, I was. And now that I am, I don't want to lose it again. I don't want to lose you." He framed her face, loving her with his fingertips, with his eyes, with every fiber of his being. "I don't want you walking out of my life."

As if she would, now. "What are you going to do to make me stay?"

It took every effort for Tony to keep his face straight. "I was thinking that, since your designs are so innovative, you might think about joining the firm." He'd already talked about this with the others, and had their enthusiastic backing. "We could be a double threat in the building industry if we had not only the construction company, but a top-notch architect as well."

"Business? This is about business?"

He gave up the joke. While it was true that his cousins wanted her to join the firm, that wasn't why he was here.

Tony laughed, hugging her. "Oh, lady, I mean business. I never meant business so much in my life. You might not realize this, but you saved me, Mikky. Saved me from becoming a petrified piece of wood inside. Until you came along, I didn't feel as though I had any emotions left at all."

"You certainly breathed fire convincingly enough."

"The first step to thawing out," he allowed with a wink. Could she tell how much she meant to him? How much he loved her? It didn't matter, he meant to spend the rest of his life showing her. "I want to make this permanent."

"You want me to be a partner in the firm?"

"I want you to be *my* partner. You can make your decision about the firm later."

It was Mikky's turn to deadpan. She did remarkably well, seeing as she wanted to shout her answer loud enough for her entire neighborhood to hear her.

"How long do I have to make up my mind and give you my answer?"

Suddenly Tony was afraid again. Afraid that after laying his soul bare, she'd back away at the last second. "I know it's a big decision—and sudden. You can take as much time as you need." *As long as you give me the right answer.*

She nodded. "That's fair." And then she raised her eyes to his. "Is now too soon?"

He was aware that he was holding his breath. "Depends."

She touched the tip of her tongue to her lip. "On what?"

He looked into her eyes and thought he knew. Or was that just wishful thinking?

"On the answer."

Her self-restraint disappeared. "How's yes?"

"Yes is terrific." His arms tightened around her. "And so are you."

"Hey, when you're right, you're right." She laughed, standing up on her toes to be closer to his mouth. "And you are right," she whispered just before he kissed her. "The right one for me."

Epilogue

"So?" Not being one to stand on ceremony, Bridgette pounced on Tony and Mikky the moment they walked in the door.

"Give them time to get their coats off, Ma," Angelo admonished.

Even as he said it, he knew it would do no good. He had to admit they were all curious as to how things had gone between Tony and Mikky. It seemed to him that the couple were the last ones to realize how good they were for each other and how good they looked together.

Impatient, Bridgette waved her hand at her son, dismissing his reprimand. "The coats they can always take off. This is important." She got in between Mikky and Tony, helping Mikky off with her coat, her eyes bright. "Did he ask you?"

Tony shrugged out of his jacket. "You know, if I hadn't already, Aunt Bridgette, you would have just ruined it for me."

She didn't see it that way. Lifting her head regally,

she countered. "No, if you hadn't, my asking would have forced you to take her aside and do it." And then she smiled broadly, looking from one to the other. "But you did do it, didn't you?" Overjoyed, she clapped her hands together. Nothing she liked better than another wedding—unless it was another baby. And now there would be both. "I can tell by that look in both your eyes. You asked and she answered, and now my family is even bigger than it was this morning." Opening her arms, she enfolded Mikky.

"You can still back out of this, you know," Shad confided to Mikky, talking to her over Bridgette's shoulder. "You don't know what you're letting yourself in for."

Bridgette released her, only to pass her on to Angelo and then Shad. It seemed as if everyone was taking a turn hugging her. Hugging him. And then they were beside each other, arms linked.

"Oh, I think I know," Mikky assured Shad. "I have a big family, too. And there's nothing in the world like it."

"No," Tony agreed, looking at her. "There's not."

Alessandra walked into the room, carrying Justin. "Someone here to see you."

Recognizing them, Justin's smile widened even more. Mikky made it to his side first. She took him into her arms. God, but he felt good. "Hi, big guy, I've missed you."

"Yeah, me, too," Tony murmured.

"Look." Alessandra pointed to the doorway. "Mistletoe."

They both looked up to see the sprig hanging down over them. Technically, it looked as if it was directly over Justin, who was between them.

Mikky smiled as she looked at Tony. "I guess we can't disappoint them."

"Them?" Tony echoed. "I was thinking of me."

As their lips met directly over Justin's downy blond head, oblivious to the sound of applause all around them, neither of them was disappointed at all. And knew they would never be again.

* * * * *

Coming in December 1999
Two award-winning authors invite
you home for the holidays!

'TIS THE
Season
by
DEBBIE
MACOMBER and
LISA JACKSON

CHRISTMAS MASQUERADE by Debbie Macomber

He'd stolen a kiss in the crowd—and taken her heart with it.
Then she met him again, engaged to another! Jo Marie
dreamed about uncovering the truth behind the engagement
and claiming Andrew for her own groom!

SNOWBOUND by Lisa Jackson

All Bethany Mills wanted for Christmas was peace and quiet.
But sexy investigator Brett Hanson stirred up the past and
then whisked her away to his mountain cabin for safety—but
from whom did she need protecting…?

Available December 1999 at your favorite retail outlet.

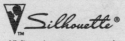

Silhouette®

Visit us at www.romance.net   PSBR21299

Temperatures rise and hearts sizzle in

TEXAS HEAT by

MARY LYNN BAXTER

Bestselling author Mary Lynn Baxter brings you three tempting stories about the power of mutual attraction.

Passions ignite when three fiery women meet the Western heroes they've always dreamed of. But will true love be found?

Find out in TEXAS HEAT, on sale November 1999 at your favorite retail outlet.

Silhouette ®

Visit us at www.romance.net

PSBR31299

The clock is ticking for three brides-to-be in these three brand-new stories!

3, 2, 1 ... Married!

In this exciting collection of romantic tales, three marriage-minded women set their sights on becoming brides in time for the New Year.

How to hook a husband when time is of the essence?

Bestselling author **SHARON SALA** takes her heroine way out west, where the men are plentiful...and more than willing to make some lucky lady a "Miracle Bride."

Award-winning author **MARIE FERRARELLA** tells the story of a single woman searching for any excuse to visit the playground and catch sight of a member of "The Single Daddy Club."

Beloved author **BEVERLY BARTON** creates a heroine who discovers that personal ads are a bit like opening Door Number 3—the prize for "Getting Personal" may just be more than worth the risk!

On sale December 1999, at your favorite retail outlet.
Only from Silhouette Books!

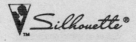

Visit us at www.romance.net   PS321

Coming from Silhouette Romance®:

Cinderella BRIDES

From rising star

ELIZABETH HARBISON

These women are about to live out their very own fairy tales...but will they live happily ever after?

On sale November 1999
EMMA AND THE EARL (SR #1410)

She thought she'd outgrown dreams of happily-ever-after, yet when American Emma Lawrence found herself a guest of Earl Brice Palliser's lavish estate, he seemed her very own Prince Charming.

On sale December 1999
PLAIN JANE MARRIES THE BOSS (SR #1416)

Sexy millionaire Trey Breckenridge III had finally asked Jane Miller to marry him. She knew he only needed a convenient wife to save his business, so Jane had just three months to show Trey the joys a forever wife could bring!

And look for the fairy tale to continue in January 2000 in **ANNIE AND THE PRINCE**.

Cinderella Brides, only from

Silhouette ROMANCE™

Available at your favorite retail outlet.

Visit us at www.romance.net

**Start celebrating Silhouette's 20th anniversary
with these 4 special titles by
New York Times bestselling authors**

Fire and Rain
by Elizabeth Lowell

King of the Castle
by Heather Graham Pozzessere

State Secrets
by Linda Lael Miller

Paint Me Rainbows
by Fern Michaels

On sale in December 1999

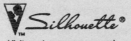

EXTRA! EXTRA!

The book all your favorite authors are raving about is finally here!

The 1999 Harlequin and Silhouette coupon book.

Each page is alive with savings that can't be beat!

Getting this incredible coupon book is as easy as 1, 2, 3.

1. During the months of November and December 1999 buy any 2 Harlequin or Silhouette books.

2. Send us your name, address and 2 proofs of purchase (cash receipt) to the address below.

3. Harlequin will send you a coupon book worth $10.00 off future purchases of Harlequin or Silhouette books in 2000.

Send us 3 cash register receipts as proofs of purchase and we will send you 2 coupon books worth a total saving of $20.00 (limit of 2 coupon books per customer).

Saving money has never been this easy.

Please allow 4-6 weeks for delivery. Offer expires December 31, 1999.

I accept your offer! Please send me (a) coupon booklet(s):

Name: _____

Address: _____ City: _____

State/Prov.: _____ Zip/Postal Code: _____

Send your name and address, along with your cash register receipts as proofs of purchase, to:

In the U.S.: Harlequin Books, P.O. Box 9057, Buffalo, N.Y. 14269
In Canada: Harlequin Books, P.O. Box 622, Fort Erie, Ontario L2A 5X3

Order your books and accept this coupon offer through our web site
http://www.romance.net
Valid in U.S. and Canada only.

PHQ4994R